House of Ravens

A Shadow Atlas Novel

Jenny Sandiford

VELIKOR
PUBLISHING

JENNY SANDIFORD

A SHADOW ATLAS NOVEL

HOUSE OF
RAVENS

Contact: jennysandiford.com

Cover designer: Miblart

Editors: Mandi Oyster and Lori Diederich

Proofreader: Amy McKenna

ISBN (ebook): 978-0-6454449-3-3

ISBN (paperback): 978-0-6454449-4-0

ISBN (hardcover): 978-0-6454449-5-7

First Edition: February 2023

To my husband, Michael, for making our lives a wonderful adventure!

Before...

Thousands of years ago, gods walked amongst the mortals of this world.

Two types of magic divided them:

Echo Magic- light magic sourced from the Echo Dimension.

Shadow Magic- dark magic sourced from the Shadow Dimension.

When it came time for humanity to stand on its own, the gods and goddesses, now known by many names, returned to their dimensions, but not without leaving their mark on the world.

The deities bestowed gifts of unique powers on chosen families around the globe, and so the Houses of Magic were created.

But over time, many of these gifts were lost. Humans, weakened by their need for power and dominance, destroyed all but eight of the great Houses.

Four Shadow Magic Houses and four Echo Magic Houses are all that remain.

Today, their legacies live on . . .

SHADOW MAGIC HOUSES

Dark Magic. Source: Shadow Dimension

HOUSE OF SNAKES
The Goddess Ereshkigal
Spirits and Necromancy

HOUSE OF WHITE DEER
The Goddess Gula
Healing Magic

HOUSE OF RAVENS
The God Zakar
Sleep and Dream Magic

HOUSE OF WINGED BULLS
The Goddess Nanna
Divination

ECHO MAGIC HOUSES

Light Magic. Source: Echo Dimension

HOUSE OF OWLS
The God Enki
Mind and Water Magic

HOUSE OF PHOENIX
The God Utu
Fire Magic

HOUSE OF EAGLES
The God Enlil
Air and Weather Magic

HOUSE OF BEES
The Goddess Ninhursag
Plant Magic

Chapter 1

Torin knew today was going to be a disaster. He thought he'd snuck out of combat training early enough to escape Kira's notice, but when he glanced over his shoulder mid-run, there she was, following him up the driveway. He stopped to wait and watched as she jogged toward him.

It was that glint in her eye as she dashed up the driveway that told him he was in for trouble. But her black training outfit, heavy military boots, and plait of shiny brown hair bouncing on her shoulder made her look like a modern-day elven princess about to embark on a quest.

Stop it, Torin. Thinking about his best friend that way was the last thing he should be doing. He should be getting on with the task his father set him, collecting much-needed ingredients for a batch of rare toxins.

Getting into his father's good books was the key to everything. Only then would his father see he was ready for his final test to level up to apprentice. Only then would he see Torin was worthy of taking revenge on his mother's murderer.

The Rook, an enormous gray castle in the English countryside, towered behind Kira like a cold stone shadow. Ravens dotted the fortress walls like tiny sentries as Torin stood as still as a statue in the wide driveway beside the walled garden.

The Rook was a lot of things: his childhood home, his future, his school, his training ground, his prison, but it was no longer home. Not since his mother died. No. Not died. Was *murdered* by the leader of the House of Snakes—The Viper. Kira was the only one who made it feel anywhere close to home now.

If he knew what was good for him, he would ignore Kira and leave without her, would use his elemer, a magical dagger, to cut into the Hollow—the sub-dimensional void between this world and the Shadow Dimension—and get on with his job.

But no, he waited like a love-struck half-wit. Why couldn't he just listen to his own good advice? His grip tightened so hard on the elemer handle that the gemstones dug into his palm. Damn his indecisiveness.

Kira skidded to a stop right in front of him. "Did you just run away from me?" She carried a black puffer jacket, same as his, which meant she knew where he was going.

"I was hoping you wouldn't notice. You may recall yesterday when I specifically told you not to come, yes?" He crossed his arms in what he hoped was a casual way, and not like he thought about her every waking moment of the day.

"Fat chance of that happening," she said.

"I gathered as much. But my father can't know, so don't screw this up for me."

"Your dad's an arsehole. But not to worry, I've got your back."

"He may be an arsehole, but he's an arsehole that everyone around here listens to."

"Except for you." She linked her arm with his and pulled him toward the entrance to the walled garden where two guards stood watch. They had no visible weapons, but they were both mages for the House of Ravens, highly trained in combat Shadow Magic, and not people you would mess with.

"I listen. I just don't always agree," Torin said.

Torin nodded to Anders, one of his favorite guards, as they stepped through the iron gates into the courtyard, the one place on the Rook's grounds without wards, hence the only place you could enter or leave the Hollow.

"You didn't see her," Torin whispered to Anders as he went past.

Anders tapped his nose in understanding. But of course, if the great and powerful Korbyn Dumont asked, he would have to answer. And speak of the devil, his father's black Rolls-Royce glided up the driveway like a sleek metallic cat full of self-importance.

"Run," Torin said.

Kira didn't need telling twice. They darted through the gate. The smell of jasmine hit him hard and fast, a sharp reminder of his mother that rattled him every time he entered the space. It had once been her garden, and without a grave to mourn her, this was the closest Torin had to a place to visit her. He didn't know what happened to her body; his father never told him.

Torin suspected his father's indifference to him was due to the painful reminder of Torin's mother, Yelena Dumont, the one thing they had in common, the one person they had both loved.

Torin had the same brown skin, dark eyes, high cheekbones, and apparently the same smile as her.

Korbyn Dumont was never a kind man, but at least when Torin's mother was alive, he wasn't cruel. It was the grief that corrupted his father's soul; it sent him into a spiral of paranoia, making him see enemies everywhere. For Torin, taking down his mother's killer wouldn't just be for revenge or setting the balance right, it was a chance to bring some sort of peace to his father, then perhaps things would be a little better for everyone.

The crunch of gravel told Torin the car had pulled up.

"Let's get out of here," Kira said, the sparkle in her eyes replaced with urgency.

"I thought you weren't worried about my father?" Torin teased, but he moved fast. Jaw clenched in focus, he raised his elemer blade high, and a rush of magic shimmered through him as the magical blade slid like butter through the subspace between this world and the Shadow Dimension.

Folding back the silky dimensional fabric with his knife, frayed shadows rippled from the darkness as Kira stepped into the Hollow first. Torin wasted no time jumping in behind her.

The sunlight turned to a single slit of blinding brightness before sealing behind him and leaving them in the low blue light of the weird spongy floor. The Hollow was a void between worlds with every direction leading into darkness. There wasn't much to it. You could walk for hours in the dark and never come across anything. Just the same dim blue light.

Unlike the Shadow Dimension, a mysterious world that Shadow Magic Houses drew their magic from; a world of ancient gods, demons, and spirits—or so the stories went. The Shadow Dimension was the source of Shadow magic and accessed by making tiny cuts between worlds to draw magic through with an elemer.

"Close one. You think he saw me?" Kira said.

The luminescent ground lit up her face with deep, eerie shadows. It only made her more beautiful, like a goddess from the Shadow Dimension. Shit, he was staring again. His eyes shot to the floor. *Stop it. She doesn't think about you that way.* He was so far into the friend zone with Kira it was hard to see himself ever clawing his way out, but it didn't mean he wouldn't try.

Unfortunately, their squad mate, Conner, appeared to have similar feelings toward Kira lately. Bloody Conner. A shame, because Torin used to like him.

"I'd bet my elemer that he saw you, knowing our rotten luck. Remember last night when I told you not to come?" Torin said. A waste of breath, he suspected.

"Too bad. I'm here now. He should never have ordered you to gather the starbells without backup."

Instead of pursuing the matter, he took in the familiar chilling air of the Hollow and put on his mask of I-know-what-I'm-doing, despite the fact that he was pretty much winging it from here.

Kira folded her arms when he remained silent. "Let's just get on with this. He won't be as pissed off if we come back with the right stuff."

She was right. Damn her. If they came back with the starbell flowers, at least he would have passed today's test.

"Fine. But be quiet so we don't end up in the middle of the sea or somewhere ridiculous," Torin said as he closed his eyes and focused his mind.

It was easy enough to cut into the Hollow, but cutting out at the right place in the world was a different story. Fortunately, he had been to this site before—Lake Khövsgöl, Mongolia. Or more precisely, a south-facing mountainside at the edge of the giant lake about 60km from the Russian border. It was one of the few places in the world this species of starbells grew, and one of the many places his father had made enemies.

Torin sliced into the blackness with his elemer. A blast of icy air tunneled into the Hollow as the doorway opened on the other side of the world.

"Easy peasy," he said, hoping it was the right place.

"Jeez, it's bloody cold," Kira said, peering around the edge of the curtain of shadowiness.

"Keen senses, this one," he teased. She was right, though. It was usually much colder inside the Hollow than outside, but in this case, it was about even. Fricken freezing.

The vibrant blue sky and blinding snow stabbed at Torin's eyes, which would now appear solid black after using his magic. He craned his head out to get a better look.

"This the right place?" Kira's chin perched on his shoulder, her warm breath gliding across his neck, and a shiver ran through him. He liked her being so close.

"Looks like it." Honestly, it was hard to tell. He had to at least make it look like he knew what he was doing. "All clear."

Kira lifted her chin and grinned at him. She was close behind as he stepped out, sinking in the crunchy snow up to his ankles. He offered a hand.

"Thank you, kind sir," Kira said with a put-on accent as she hopped down next to him.

He wished he could respond cleverly but just said, "You're welcome," like an idiot. The skin of her palm was soft but had the same callouses as his own, callouses that molded perfectly to their elemers. The Hollow sealed, leaving them alone in the Siberian wilderness.

Torin took a breath of crisp, pine-scented air as Kira bounced on her toes, taking in the view. Tiny wisps escaped her braid and danced in the light breeze; he held back the urge to touch her hair.

"This is all it takes to shut you up?" he said.

She rolled her eyes but didn't stop smiling.

Torin adjusted his backpack, checking it was still there. This was the right place. Way below, the massive ice lake stretched farther than he could see, its icy blue finish looking like a cracked mirror from above. Tree branches rustled and birds chattered away in the evening sun. It was spring here, but the ice stuck around long past winter, growing thinner with every day. When Torin was little, they used to come here as a family and stay with the local shamans to trade for starbells and other rare plants. He had loved to lie on the ice and listen to its music as it melted and remembered his mother lying right there next to him, her long hair spread out around her and her laughter singing out across the frozen lake.

"It's gorgeous," Kira said.

Torin forced himself away from the view. They shouldn't be wasting time; he wasn't on a date for gods' sake. There were shamans in the area who happened to be highly trained mages—mages who hated his father and wouldn't hesitate to attack if they found intruders on their mountain. His eyes wandered. They probably had wards set up to alert them to unwanted guests.

"Get your arse into gear." Torin nudged Kira with the butt of his elemer, and she went to hit him back, but he moved too quickly.

"Twat," she called after him as he set off.

He led the way across the uneven slope, crunching through slushy snow and mud, bringing them closer to the edge of the woods. He aimed for the rounded boulders the size of small elephants.

"This spot looks fine," Torin said, shrugging off his backpack and setting it down on a patch of dry grass by a sunny rock where the snow had melted away. He pulled out two pairs of latex gloves and tossed one set to Kira—lucky he had spares; starbells were highly toxic. This was the extent of his romantic gestures.

Even to him, it was clear he had zero chance against Conner, who always knew the right thing to say around girls.

"You search that end of the rock. I'll start at the other. Be careful, right?" he said as he slipped on the gloves.

"I've read the procedures," she said with an eye roll.

Of course, she knew what she was doing.

They worked in silence for about ten minutes, carefully brushing away snow to reveal the valuable flowers tucked into the brown grass. The plants were distinctive, each with four minty-green, lamb-ear-like leaves with a central stalk containing their prize: a white bell-shaped flower with a collar of green that made a tiny star. Careful not to touch it, Torin snipped the top of each flower off into a sandwich bag.

Kira appeared deep in concentration, using a pair of tweezers to free a stalk from beneath the dry grass.

A couple of birds landed on top of the rock.

"Great tits," Torin said, glancing at Kira while suppressing a smile.

"Say what?" Kira sat up and shot him a look.

Torin tried to keep a straight face. "Great tits—those birds." He nodded to the round green and yellow passerines with glossy black heads and white cheeks. She fell for it every time.

"Real mature, Tor." He could hear the eye roll without even looking at her. Worth it.

The forest erupted in an explosion of birds from the tree line as a low rumble vibrated across the mountainside. Torin tilted his head in the direction it was coming from.

"Shit, we've got company," Kira whispered.

"They don't know where we are. Starbells grow all over this mountain," he answered back, doing his best to sound confident. He'd always come here with guards or his father, people who had experience fighting. It would have been easier if it was just him. Putting Kira at risk was the last thing he wanted, but now wasn't the time for *I-told-you-so*'s.

Kira crouched motionless with her hand resting on the boulder, eyes focused on the trees.

"They're close. Grab a few more flowers, and we'll head out once they pass," he said, hoping they would, in fact, pass by.

For once, Kira didn't argue. She hurried along the edge of the stone as Torin did the same. They couldn't come back empty-handed—better to not come back at all.

The sweat pooling in Torin's gloves did not help the situation. *Must keep collecting starbells.* He angled his body lower as the roar of motorbikes grew louder. They were heading right for them.

"Shit. Let's get out of here," Torin said, making the executive decision.

"Just a few more. This isn't even enough to make one batch of toxin," Kira said.

Trust Kira to want to keep going. She had always been the risk taker, ever since he'd met her that first day when her parents dropped her at the Rook, handing their little girl over to train as a soldier or assassin with smiles on their faces. He didn't know how they could do that.

She was so pleased to be there, she'd wanted to go straight to the highest level of the obstacle course when they were ten. Torin was happy to stay on the first level until he mastered it. But he'd followed her and always would. That's the way it worked between them, her pushing and Torin excelling because of her.

Torin yanked away grass and snipped off starbells like a madman as the drone of engines drilled into his brain like a swarm of converging bees. The deep bellow of indistinguishable men's voices was close. Too close.

"Enough. Get up."

Kira kept going as Torin stood.

Two bikes shot out from the tree line, hurtling up the mountain, snow and mud flicking up like dirt confetti behind them.

"Stop!" a man yelled in Mongolian.

Torin knew enough of the language to understand the word, though he didn't need to know any to recognize how pissed off this guy was. His round face had veins ready to burst out of his forehead.

More bikes exploded from the trees—at least four, too many to handle on their own. Two guys on the backs of the bikes were aiming rifles.

"Duck!" Torin yelled, throwing himself to the ground next to Kira as shards of rock splintered around them from gunshots. With the stealth of a lioness, Kira crept to the other side of the rock and peered around.

"They're closing in," she hissed.

This was the sort of thing they trained for, and there was always a way out. They would have to go into the forest.

Chapter 2

"**P**ack up the flowers. I'll distract them," Torin said as a blast of heat rushed past him. It was a freaking fireball, and it barely missed his head. *Okay, so they had fire mages, wonderful.* The flaming ball bounced a few meters away, smoldering and crackling as it ate up the dry grass.

Slashing into the air with his elemer blade, Torin spun the knife 180 degrees to flick the key out the other end. He drew magic from the Shadow Dimension through the key and up through the magical knife edge, forcing it into his body. At the same time, he formed a spell cloud in his mind, summoning power symbols into the swirling blue cloud of magic, adding in energy and intent as he went.

This was the magic of the House of Ravens, one of the eight Houses of Magic and one of the four that practiced Shadow Magic. The powers were a gift to his ancestors thousands of years ago from the god Zakar, the god of dreams. Zakar gave them the power to control sleep and dreams, as well as the ability to harness the shadows, manipulate them, and use them to fight or conceal themselves as they wished.

With a deep breath, Torin collected the magic and pushed it back out his elemer. The air filled with the smell of Shadow Magic, electrical and alive like the heart of a thunderstorm.

Sweeping the elemer blade in a horizontal arc, he blanketed the world in front of him in thick shadows. The wall was dense enough to stop bullets and, hopefully, these people for a short while.

Kira was onto it. Fast as a fox, she appeared at his side, already cutting into the Hollow with her elemer. Flames sprung out of the grass, lashing out at them with long unnatural fingers, and they both ducked.

"Great. A fire mage," Kira said.

"We can take them," Torin said with false confidence.

Fire magic was a nightmare to fight with shadows. The mages would be from the House of Phoenix, and instead of Shadow Magic, they used the opposite—Echo Magic. A light magic they drew from the Echo Dimension.

Torin threw his arm up to shield his face at a pulse of unexpected heat. It blasted into the sky, licking at the trees as if someone had poured petrol on it. The heat melted his concentration away. Kira must have felt it too, because the shadow door to the Hollow sealed shut before they could get through.

A man as big as a bear sliced through Torin's weakening shadow wall. Flames blasted from his elemer like a flamethrower. *Yup, time to run.*

Kira yanked Torin away as a fireball shot dangerously close to his ear. Her eyes were solid black. It made her look powerful.

"On your feet, Dumont," she ordered, sounding shockingly like Mage Emerson during training.

It snapped him into gear, and he ran. Sprinting through the snow, he followed Kira in the opposite direction of the men and straight into the dense forest. At least the bikes wouldn't be able to get into the thick underbrush she was heading for.

"This is our forest. You cannot hide," a man bellowed behind them in heavily accented English, but he sounded far away already.

I am well aware of that and more than happy to get the fuck out of here. Torin pelted down a steep slope, skidding through patches of snow and pine needles until he stabilized himself in a semi-graceful slide. They could run forever if they had to, but those blokes chasing them would be slow wearing bulky *deels*, traditional Mongolian outfits made of sheepskin and thick wool—warm, but hard to move in. They wouldn't catch up.

"Heads up!" Kira yelled.

Fireballs rained down like arrows in a medieval battle. Torin wove and dodged as many as he could, but from the smell of melting plastic, some must have hit his jacket.

"Get to the other side of that outcrop down there. It should cover us long enough to open into the Hollow," Torin yelled.

Pain grazed across his cheek as Kira let out a scream, and Torin's heart plummeted to his feet. He skidded to a halt and took two great leaps to catch up with Kira. Scrambling across the slushy snow, he crouched next to her sprawled form in a mixture of mud and pine needles.

She turned her head, and he couldn't help but wince. The side of her face was blistered and raw from a fireball hit. He put his hand to his own cheek; it was barely singed.

"Up, Kiri. We have to keep moving," he said using her childhood nickname.

Torin grabbed a handful of snow and pressed it to her cheek as she sucked in a pained breath.

"That fucker," she hissed, but nodded and forced herself up.

Heavy footsteps thudded down the hill behind them.

"They're here."

Their attackers were too close to open into the Hollow anywhere near here. Hoisting Kira up by her elbow, he forced her into a run. Trees whipped past them as they stumbled down the steep slope. Fire blasted through the trees, and the sting of burning resin hung in the air as flakes of ash tumbled around them like snow.

Then everything was upside down. Torin was flying. Fireballs whizzed past in flashes of orange and white as he crashed through a rotting log and tumbled into a—sort of—controlled roll a short way down the hill. Panting, he got up, but it was lost time. A fireball must have hit the ground behind him.

"Keep moving," Kira yelled, but it was too late.

The two men skidded to a halt in front of them. Panting for breath, the men stood tall, both with a lust for blood in their eyes. Massive biceps threatened to split their sleeves, and their hands looked like they could crush a skull. Okay, so maybe Torin had underestimated them. They had certainly kept up, having both shed their *deels*, and now wore jeans and long-sleeved wool shirts all covered in sweat and singe marks. Fire mages.

"House of Ravens," one said in a thick Russian accent as he spat on the ground in front of them. Torin and Kira stood back-to-back as the two men circled them like wolves. The one who spoke was definitely a fire mage, judging from the fireball in his hand. Torin wasn't sure about the other man, but he held a rifle.

"We don't want to hurt you," Kira said.

"You killed our shaman." The fire mage threw a fireball over their head, leaving his hands sparking with angry embers.

Torin's heart froze, knowing the shaman—that sweet old man who showed him where to find wild strawberries in summer—was dead.

"That wasn't us," Torin said, but of course, he knew who was responsible—his father. The very thought of it turned his stomach. Torin had known the shaman since he was a boy. The times when his father left him alone, the shaman taught him how to listen to the trees, how to forage for medicinal plants, and how to control the world inside his dreams. This was back when the mages in the area were allied with their family.

Did his father really have no limits? This was why he needed to leave. As soon as he got justice, he was gone. He would leave his father and all this misery behind. He just had to convince Kira to come with him somehow.

"We won't be able to reason with them," Kira hissed under her breath.

Torin knew this was true. He didn't want to fight or hurt them, but he also knew they wouldn't hesitate to get their revenge, whether he was the murderer or not.

"We can take them," Torin said under his breath, not taking his eyes off the men.

He hoped Kira wouldn't be a liability with her injury. They had to be fast and precise. No mistakes. No second chances, as his father so often reminded them.

"Three, two, one," he counted so only Kira could hear, then flicked his elemer out, blasting thick ropes of shadows out in front of him and relishing the surge of pure magic. The shadows curled out like black, undulating tentacles and seized the mage. Breathing deep to maintain the spell, Torin raised his arms, and the shadowy ropes surged high into the trees. The man's leg kicked out wildly beneath him.

Pivoting around, he saw Kira had done the same to the other man. *Nicely done.* The gun clattered to the ground.

Beads of sweat prickled at Torin's forehead with the strain of the spell. The man struggled, hands spitting fire in pathetic bursts, but not enough to break himself free. He'd need his elemer to do that, and Torin could see it glinting with reflected flames several feet away on a tree root.

"Hold tight. I'll open the Hollow," Kira yelled as she tied the gunman to the tree like a fly in a shadowy spider's web.

Torin didn't speak for fear of losing concentration on his spell, holding the mage high in the air. He was the one they needed to watch. After several long seconds, Torin nearly tripped when Kira's hand wrapped around his arm.

"My guy's stuck to a tree. On the count of three, come straight back," Kira said.

Torin could smell the icy breeze from the Hollow; it was clean and pure compared to the burning forest and earthy snow slush. He trusted Kira. He nodded.

"One, Two, Three—"

Torin released his spell, and the fire mage plummeted straight down, but Torin didn't stop to watch. He turned, about to follow Kira into the Hollow, but a deafening crack broke the stillness of the forest.

His shoulder slammed forward. *What the hell?* Twisting around in shock, Torin's eyes darted around the trees. He was sure someone had hit him, but no one was there.

"Torin! Behind you," Kira called out. She ducked, and the Hollow closed.

Torin twisted around to see the gunman charging at him like a raging dragon. He'd freed himself from the tree somehow. Kira reacted fast and darted into the trees.

All logical thinking was out the window; it was survival mode now. Standing his ground, Torin braced himself as the man plowed toward him. There was no time to move.

Where was Kira? He spun around. The other mage had gotten up and was hot on Kira's heels. She dodged between two trees, unable to lose him. He was quick. Torin sprinted toward them, but he was already too far behind.

Terror rose in his chest. What if something happened to her? It would all be his fault, and he would never forgive himself. His legs burned as he pushed forward, all the while watching the man get closer to Kira.

She spun around, probably knowing she couldn't outrun him.

"Keep running," Torin screamed with what little air was burning in his lungs, burning from running and from the smoke building around him.

The air grew thick, and he lost sight of them; then a scream cut through the haze. He ran straight for it.

Magic gathered in his blood, fueled by anger and fear, surging him forward.

"Kira!" he called, his voice hoarse and dry.

BANG. A gunshot. He was sure of it.

He changed course again, weaving through the trees, his ears straining to find any movement in the thickening smoke from the burning undergrowth and low branches around him. The trail of flames followed him. It seemed both men were fire mages.

Torin followed the newly lit branches, and a muffled cry came from his left. Then thundering hooves shook the ground.

He stumbled into a clearing filled with horses darting for the trees—unexpected, but he ignored them and scanned the area.

Near the center of the meadow was a rotting tree stump with Kira crumpled at the bottom. The fire mage had a glowing ball of flames in his hand and was panting heavily as he stood with his foot pressed into Kira's chest as she flailed under it.

Red flashed across Torin's vision. "Get off her!" He charged forward.

His blood heated like it was boiling as every muscle in his body sprang into action.

Around him, horses thundered by, too close for comfort, their breath steaming into the frigid air, and their snorts and frightened warnings to one another bellowed around him.

Torin charged at full speed, anger pounding through his veins, pumping up his magic. He didn't slow down as he propelled all his weight straight into the mage.

The impact rattled Torin's bones, and he met the hard earth, slamming all the air from his lungs. Gasping for breath, he couldn't move.

He didn't have time to breathe or work out where Kira was. The man was on top of him, straddling him with the gun aimed at his chest.

Torin strained to fill his lungs; he couldn't think. But he had gotten the man away from Kira, at least. She could get away.

Torin instinctively pushed his hand hard into his attacker's chest.

Power symbols he had never seen before appeared in his mind, and he drew in magic from the surrounding air without even thinking or using his elemer. The man's pulse was strong beneath his palm; he could hear it like a steady drum.

Anger thrummed in Torin's chest. Why had his father killed their shaman? Why couldn't he have protected Kira better?

Why couldn't these men leave him alone so he wouldn't have to hurt them?

His usual control was out the window. He was no better than his ten-year-old self. Blinded by rage, he allowed a spell cloud to develop in his mind, uncontrolled. One power symbol grew clearer; its sharp lines formed a backward Z with the spine straight up and down and the arms tilted inward with three bars across the middle. It wasn't familiar.

Then, with the ease of a breath, the magic released in a surge of furious white energy and seared right into the man's chest above him.

Everything went still. There was a heartbeat beneath his fingers one second, then it stopped.

The roar of anger in his blood dissipated. The trees no longer moved, and the birds were silent. He couldn't hear the wild horses, or maybe it was the blood pounding in his ears that blocked it all out.

Torin rolled the man off him and sat up, gasping. Something wasn't right. He stared at his hand, and a throb of pain registered in his shoulder. Time stood still as a roaring grew in his ears.

"Get up!" Kira screamed.

Torin shook himself out of his daze and scrambled to his feet as the other fire mage came at them, recovered from his fall and apparently good at tracking.

"We need to go now!" She was standing by a door to the Hollow she must have just cut.

The mage lumbered toward him. His face fell as he spotted his friend. "What did you do?"

Torin stumbled toward Kira. She pulled him into the Hollow, and he fell onto the soft blue ground. Its moss-like tentacles tickled his cheek as if they were welcoming him home.

The Hollow sealed shut.

Kira collapsed next to him, lying on her back. Her face was a mess, and her hair was tangled with forest debris, but she was smiling as her chest rose and fell, catching her breath.

"You okay?" he asked, leaning up on his elbows.

"I should be asking you that. You got shot," she said.

"I did?" Torin brought his hand to his shoulder. It came away sticky with blood, and a slow burn grew with his awareness. That explained that feeling of getting hit earlier, at least. "Ow. I didn't expect that to be a bullet."

"Trust you not to notice getting shot." She shook her head and looked down at her hands. "But thanks for the save. I owe you one."

"You don't owe me anything. I wasn't about to leave you on the other side of the world with murderous fire mages."

"Your dad would expect you to. It was my fault I got caught."

"I'm not my father, and I'll never leave you behind. I promise."

"Good to know." A smile parted her lips.

A heavy silence settled across the Hollow. They should probably get out of there. Maybe a change in subject . . .

"You got hit with a fireball. Are you okay?" Torin sat up and let his hand hover near Kira's face as she raised herself on her elbows. Her injury was far worse than his.

"It's fine," she said.

He traced the smooth skin of her jawline with his fingers, away from the burn. His shoulder was screaming like someone had stuck a hot poker in there. "I wish I knew healing magic," he said, studying her face. How did she remain so calm? It must be the pain. That, or the adrenaline was blocking it.

"Don't let your dad catch you saying that." She sat up and pulled her knees to her chest.

"I think I killed that man," he said. *No, correction, I definitely killed that man.*

"How? I didn't see, but he certainly looked dead."

"I put my hand on his chest, and he died." Torin's heart raced just thinking about it. Had he really killed him?

Kira raised her eyebrows and tilted her head. "Like the hand of death from our book?"

"I don't know. It sounds ridiculous when you say it out loud. It's just a silly myth."

"But what if it's real? No one has had the hand of death for centuries. Imagine what your dad will say."

"He'd want to use me for it."

"Or you could use it yourself. You could finally take down the Viper, avenge your mother's death."

If true, that would make his task a lot easier, and his father might set him the task sooner rather than later. But it wasn't a gift he wanted to be stuck with. He'd only ever wanted to kill the one man. Set the balance right and then move on with his life in peace, away from all this craziness. But there was always a catch.

"But remember what happened to the people in the myth?" Torin asked.

"Mostly they lived." Kira shrugged.

"The prophecies say the hand of death brings some sort of destruction to the world."

"A coincidence perhaps? They're just stories. It makes them sound better that way, Tor."

"Perhaps." He didn't want to think about it. Myths always had a shred of truth in them. The question was, did he believe in children's stories enough to think the world might be destroyed because of him? If the gift was real, that is.

He stood up, a little dizzy from the pain. Silently wishing he didn't have to go back to the Rook, he shut his eyes. That probably wasn't right, wanting to stay in the Hollow with a bullet wound rather than go home.

"Come on. We should get going." He felt Kira's eyes on him.

"Don't look so guilty, Tor. You defended us. It's what we're trained to do. Get yourself together so we can go back," she said, easing herself up.

Kira cut out of the Hollow, and the crack of light proved it was still morning in England. The sun was shining, and the doves were making annoying dove noises. Life was normal, or as normal as it could be at the House of Ravens' compound.

Torin hauled himself up and stepped past Kira into the garden, and she followed as the door to the Hollow closed. A gasp escaped his lips when he saw Kira's face in the light—it was much worse, all bubbled and seeping, and with her eyes all solid black from using magic it made her look like a demon of some sort. A wave of guilt crashed over him as he held his hand over the sticky bullet hole in his shoulder.

"You did not follow orders." The blunt voice cut right through him, and he spun around.

Torin turned to meet his father's narrow, untrusting gaze. Of course, he had been waiting. Waiting for Torin to return, waiting for him to fail, waiting so he could be there to point it out.

Torin and Kira stepped into line, hands at their sides, backs straight. Korbyn Dumont, Head of the House of Ravens, marched in front of them. Torin was tall, about a head taller than his father, but somehow the man held an air of power about him that Torin wished he could replicate.

Torin looked nothing like his father. They were opposites in every way, Torin was tall, dark, and quiet. His father was thin and wiry with graying hair and skin as pale as moonlight. His voice wasn't loud, but he could overpower any conversation. He was a man who used fear to control, whereas Torin preferred to lurk in the shadows and shy away from responsibility and authority.

With his raven's head cane at his side, Korbyn looked Kira up and down slowly. Another thing to add to Torin's list of things to hate him for.

Kira glared at him as if matching his challenge instead of staring straight ahead as they were trained to do.

Stupid girl. She knew better than to push his buttons.

"You two, my office now," he barked as he spun on his heels and marched through the gate without acknowledging either of the guards.

Torin and Kira darted a look at each other but didn't dare speak. Hopefully, Kira would keep her mouth shut once they got inside.

The march across the driveway was slow. The ravens above the doorway stared down like creepy gargoyles. Licorice, the raven Torin hand-raised from a chick, let out a friendly croak of greeting. Torin liked to think she had his back. Though you could never be sure with ravens.

As they neared the cold stone entrance, Torin felt his freedom slipping away once more. One thing was for sure: his father would not see this mission as a success.

Chapter 3

They marched toward the Rook—a hellhole of a place to grow up. The very air fizzed with Shadow Magic and smelled of electrical storms mingling with fresh spring air.

Even Torin's love of history couldn't tempt him to like the old fortress. The original 14th-century tower lorded over them like a giant stone box, all gray and cold. It was adorned with jagged ramparts and well equipped with all the wooden shutters and drafty hallways a castle could ever need.

He suppressed a shudder. It was never a good feeling entering the place, and nothing about it felt like home now.

Her feet crunched across the gravel next to him, no hint of pain or concern in her expression, her eyes still swirling with inky blackness from using her magic.

He pulled up his mask of confidence. He had no idea how his father would react to Kira coming along, or the fact that he had killed a man. Would the great Korbyn Dumont even believe it when it hardly seemed real to Torin?

He imagined grabbing her hand and running away there and then, just like he did in his dreams. But in his dreams, she actually ran away with him. In *those* dreams he could control everything with magic—in real life, not so much.

She would never leave the House of Ravens and the future they could offer her as a spy, a soldier, or an assassin for his father; the money and prestige were too good to turn down. Like the others in their squad, she had been left there by her family with the expectation to become the best—the best in shadow magic, the best fighter, the best strategist, another prodigy of the great Korbyn Dumont.

But Torin hadn't given up hope he could convince her to leave with him when the time came. There was more to life than this world of deceit and building armies to challenge other Houses of Magic. The crazy part was the House of Snakes, their enemies, had magic similar to the House of Ravens; the only difference was the Ravens had power over dreams and sleep, whereas the Snakes could communicate with spirits and in the past perform necromancy, though it was illegal now. It made no sense that they should be trapped in archaic feuds.

If leaving meant hiding for the rest of his life, Torin was willing to do so. Just as long as he could fulfill his promise to his mother.

Torin was so lost in thought he nearly tripped up the uneven stair that jumped out. The hallway of dark furniture, ugly statues, and threadbare tapestries swallowed them in its dim light as they left the sweet smell of spring outside.

Torin glanced at Kira to get her attention and looked down, tapping two fingers against his leg—their squad's silent signal to pay attention or stay alert. He wished they'd had time to talk before this interrogation. But before he could even think, they had turned down the next hallway, this one lined with rusting suits of armor, and were at the door to his father's office.

They stepped inside, and the door slammed.

Portraits of former masters of the Rook glared down at them from dark wood panels, all ancestors and all-powerful shadow mages. The room smelled of old cigar smoke, coffee, and aging leather.

Korbyn Dumont leaned on the back of his leather chair. "A simple task, boy, that's all it was. Flower picking on a mountain, and you botched it. I did not send you on a picnic with your girlfriend. I sent you on a mission to collect much-needed resources, so how did you fuck it up this time?"

The bullet wound pulsed at the same rate as the headache building in Torin's temples. His father stood behind his desk, behind him the ever-present family sword, its hilt gilded with rubies and a House of Ravens crest. Torin also knew it was a fake, though he'd never say it aloud to anyone. It was clearly made of silver, a useless material for a sword of any sort. It was far too soft.

"Your son got shot, and you don't even care! He needs medical attention, not a lecture," Kira said, standing with her shoulders back, hands clasped behind her and a defiant look in her eyes that had now swirled back to emerald green.

"Pathetic. You can't even speak for yourself. And you, deary." He glared at Kira. "Why were you there?"

"I was there to help." She glared right back.

Korbyn narrowed his eyes at her before a flick of his elemer sent a stream of shadows straight for her neck. Her legs flailed as the shadows lifted her like a rag doll hung at the throat.

"A week of cleaning the weapons and training gear before dawn every morning should help you think things over for the next time you want to defy orders," Korbyn said in an eerily calm voice and dropped her before Torin could react.

Kira stood up straight away, rubbing her throat and glaring at Korbyn. She was smart enough to keep her lips shut at that point.

"None of that matters now. They attacked us on the mountain," Torin said. He stood with shoulders back, fingers in a white-knuckled grasp behind him and eyes straight ahead, consciously looking past his father because if he caught his eye, he would be tempted to punch him in the face for what he just did to Kira.

"I see you're both wounded but still alive, so it can't have been too serious," Korbyn said as he pulled out his chair and settled into it.

Kira shifted between her feet. She would be itching to retaliate, but that wouldn't help either of them.

"I got shot," Torin said blankly. "And Kira needs to fix her face up."

"Tell me what happened. Were there mages? What did they want?" he said, ignoring Torin's comment.

"Two fire mages. They said their shaman was killed. Did you do it?" Torin added as his frustration built up.

"You may be my son, but I will not share privileged information with a lowly recruit, not until you prove yourself worthy."

Course he bloody well wouldn't. More cover-ups and excuses for doing whatever the fuck he wanted. Torin tried to block out the memory of the fire mage's pulse slowing against his hand. The drum of that last beat was seared into his mind like a horrific song he couldn't get out of his head.

Was he just as bad as his father now? Was he going to turn into a power-hungry madman? It was in his blood, after all.

Torin glanced at Kira's clenched fists pressed into her sides. He could almost feel the rage bubbling off her. She should be grateful he hadn't done worse; even so, they needed to get out of there ASAP before she said or did something stupid.

"Here. We collected your bloody flowers. Do your own dirty work next time," Torin said. He pulled the bag of flowers from his singed and beaten-up backpack and tossed it in front of his father on the desk. He caught Kira's eye and tilted his head toward the door.

"Don't turn your back on me," Korbyn said in a low growl.

Torin didn't turn around. He looked straight ahead and made for the door, but Kira spun around, facing Korbyn.

"We could have died, you know. All because you sent him alone, and you had to have known they would attack him. It was two blasted fire mages!" she said with a wince of pain but regained composure quickly and kept on going. "But he proved you wrong, didn't he?" Kira said with her nose in the air.

"Alright, time to go." Torin steered Kira toward the door.

"He took down two fire mages. You should be proud." Kira said.

"Did you now?" His father sounded almost amused.

Torin pivoted. Might as well bring this up now if it would hurry his chances to perform his final test. He had passed a big milestone today. He knew he could kill someone. A horrible thing to need to know, but a weight off his mind. He swallowed, wondering if this was the right time to bring it up.

"I killed one mage," he said, not feeling like the words came from his own mouth.

"You killed someone?"

"Yes."

"Recruit Reid, can you confirm this as truth?" Korbyn turned to Kira, all business.

"Yes, sir. The man had overpowered me, but Torin got him. Torin used the hand of death," Kira said, almost in awe.

Torin cringed. He hadn't wanted to use that term, not until he knew what he'd actually done.

His father chuckled, a deep and unnerving laugh. "Did you now, boy?"

"I don't know what I did, Father. I tackled the bloke, but he got the upper hand on me. I put my hand on him, and his heart slowed down until I could barely feel it. Then it just stopped."

His father stood from his desk and came around the other side. Torin turned to face him, hands clenched tight behind his back once more as Kira shuffled behind him.

"You used your hand, not the elemer?"

Torin shrugged. "Yeah, I guess so."

"You guess so, or you know so? Which is it?"

"I know so," Torin said.

"Perhaps I should give you more credit, boy. Though it's unlikely it was the hand of death. Perhaps it was the sleeping beauty curse, and the heart was merely slowed. Either way, it is advanced magic and rather impressive if true."

Of course his father wouldn't believe it was the hand of death. Who would? He wouldn't have believed it himself unless he saw it, or felt it happen.

"What was it you did exactly?" Korbyn asked.

"I killed him. I'm sure I stopped his heart with my hand. I felt it."

"Interesting . . ." Korbyn said slowly, then stepped back and ran his hand through his thin beard as if in contemplation. *Weird.* His father never liked to show he was thinking. It was always decisive action and instant commands.

"Few have the gift to slow a heart, but to stop it entirely is unheard of, rare indeed . . . if true." His gaze fell on Torin as if he was trying to read his mind. Thankfully, that was a magical skill neither of them possessed.

The blood drained from Torin's face. He knew what was coming next: he would have to prove it.

"It might not have been," he said, backtracking. "It was a fluke in the heat of the moment, and I had a power spike. That's the only reason it worked."

I wanted to kill the man for touching Kira, he chose not to add. He didn't need to give his father more fuel against him.

"If only I had a mind mage here to pry the truth from your skull."

Called it. "I consider myself fortunate you don't. But it is the truth, Father."

What sort of arsehole father says shit like that? From what Torin had read, having a mind mage force themselves into your head was the worst kind of violation and torture imaginable. His father must be trying to scare him and still didn't believe him.

"I suppose you think this makes you worthy to undertake your apprentice test?"

"Yes. I do," Torin said. Even if it wasn't true, he would have said yes. A good thing there wasn't a mind mage around.

"I will consider it if you can prove this magic you claim is real. You will meet me in one hour in the south tower."

"How will you tell if it's real or not?"

"I will test you, boy. No more questions," Korbyn snapped. "You are both dismissed. Neither of you are to accept full healing until I say so. Get Mrs. Young to patch you up. You will learn from the pain."

Torin didn't need telling twice and was out the door with Kira right behind him as they marched in silence up the hallway and out of earshot.

So, that was all it took for his father to notice him? Nearly dying and an affinity for mysterious advanced magic he didn't know he could do?

Kira nudged his side, and he winced, glimpsing the seeping flesh on her face. They really needed to get down to the kitchen for some healing.

"What are you going to do? Can you do it again do you think?" Kira asked.

"I don't know. I didn't expect him to outright bring up doing my apprenticeship test," Torin said, hoping he hadn't made a wrong move. If he couldn't do it again, he was in deep shit, but more worrying was *how* he was going to do it again. His stomach twisted at the thought of what test his father might devise for this. No doubt he was researching the hand of death right now.

"I know you can do it, Tor." She gave him a light punch on his good shoulder as they walked. "This is what we've been training for since we were ten. You'll be the one to take down the Viper; I know it. Plus, you'll be the first to be accepted as an apprentice!" She almost looked giddy but winced in pain. Kira wasn't usually one to squeal and get all emotional, but if not for the burn on her face, he suspected she might do one of those things. Maybe both.

The problem was, he'd told her he would leave as soon as he made apprentice, but she didn't believe he would go through with it. Why couldn't she see there was another way?

"Don't you just wish we were normal sometimes?" he asked.

Kira snorted. "No. Why would I want that?"

Torin frowned. "Your face is burnt, and I have a bullet in my shoulder. This shouldn't be normal."

She shrugged. "What's fun about normal? What do normal people even do?"

How about studying what they want, following their passions, studying necromancy and the dark history of magic for fun—all theoretical of course—playing video games . . . going on dates? But he didn't say any of that.

"Not kill people," he said, far more solemnly than he meant to.

She looked at him sideways as if to say, *who are you?*

He pulled on her hand to make her stop, then let it drop quickly when she faced him, too scared to see how easy it might be to sense her heartbeat. Her brow furrowed.

"I've told you I want to leave, Kira, and I mean it. I'm going to take down the Viper, get justice for my mum, and hopefully we will all be even and it will end this stupid war with my father and the House of Snakes. Maybe they can start over again, and I can start over too," he said, hoping it was true.

"You don't mean it. I know you, Torin; you can't walk away from all this. You're your father's heir. You'll be head of the House of Ravens one day. You're not stupid enough to throw that away."

He took a breath and chose his words carefully, consciously keeping his smoldering anger under control. He didn't want to argue with her again. It was clear now wasn't the time to convince her to leave.

"I wouldn't consider it a loss. This isn't the life I want with things the way they are."

"I'm not talking to you about this again. It's a rebellious phase, Tor. You're nearly sixteen; it's normal. End of conversation." She let out a huff and marched down to the kitchens ahead of him, toward the smell of baking bread and something with garlic.

This was the problem with always hiding your emotions. When someone needed to see the true you, it was hidden away with no evidence to back you up.

They were supposed to be trained for this, trained to murder people and not care. But the reality of it was a different story because today he had killed a man. He hadn't even allowed himself to feel what that meant yet—probably not good, he supposed—but who knew. He'd have to wait for that to hit later, or maybe it was this easy. And knowing that made this so much worse.

He couldn't spend his life hunting his father's enemies and not even caring if he took lives. That was not him. That was not his future.

Still, the exception would be taking down the Viper; that kill would be a pleasure. That was the one kill he dreamed of making.

He trailed after Kira. Hopefully, Mrs. Young had something that could help Kira with the pain and make sure her face didn't get infected. Healing without magic really was horrid.

Each step downstairs jarred the blood in Torin's shoulder. *Don't faint in front of Kira,* he told himself, the fuzzy effects of dizziness washing over him as the whirling sounds of industrial dishwashers grew closer. Just a few more steps to the kitchen and a chance to sit down.

They made it to the solid farmhouse table where Kira was already perched at the end. He rather liked this table; it took up the entire center of the industrial-style kitchen. It was one of the few places he had good memories of as a child, sitting there watching the cooks work while his mother would pour tea and he fed scraps to the dogs. The table was scratched up with knife cuts from what Torin assumed was a few centuries of wear and tear—a solid beast, much like Mrs. Young, the cook who eyed Torin as he walked in.

Mrs. Young was a stocky matron of a woman complete with a floral apron and a no-nonsense bun of graying hair. She liked everyone to think she was tough, but Torin had seen her soft side more than once. Well, twice, in fact. Once when his mother died, and once when his father had gone a little too far in his first year of training. Torin ended up with two broken arms after his father threw him across the room when he failed to channel magic for a "sufficient" amount of time. Mrs. Young had not only healed him but made him remember there was occasionally kindness in the world.

Torin sank into a chair opposite Kira who was biting her lip and staring at the table like she might cry. Not that he had ever seen her cry before. Still, there was a first time for everything, and he suspected the adrenaline was wearing off. Torin held on to his shoulder, trying to remain upright.

He couldn't look at Kira without feeling sick, physically sick, because her face looked dreadful—not that he would ever say that aloud—but also because of the thought of her turning her back on him when he left. And the blood loss probably wasn't helping the situation.

Instead of thinking, he focused on the red brick walls of the familiar room. They were covered with steel shelves and racks of copper pots and pans. Above them hung bushels of herbs and various plants, and of course, to the side was Mrs. Young's calendar with pictures of show dogs. This month was a Scottish terrier.

"What in Gula's name happened to you two?" Mrs. Young demanded without a hint of sympathy as she wiped her hands on her apron. Mrs. Young was from the House of the White Deer, and their goddess was the great healer Gula, as Mrs. Young liked to remind them often. She marched around the table and took Kira's chin, tilting her face toward the light and squinting at her burns. Torin looked away at a bowl of wild mushrooms that must have been recently picked.

"We were sent on a task. It did not go well." Kira winced as Mrs. Young prodded her face with a cotton swab.

"Actually, *I* was sent on a task. Kira invited herself," Torin said, hoping to distract Kira from the pain and lighten the mood. She didn't so much as look at him.

"Keep whatever it was to yourselves. I don't care, and I don't want to know," Mrs. Young said with a huff as she shuffled her large frame back to the other side of the table and began rummaging through the kitchen drawers. "Let me get my healer's supplements, and I'll get started on Miss Reid first. What's wrong with you, lad?"

"You won't need the supplements, Mrs. Young. Mage Dumont said we weren't to be healed with magic, and Tor got shot in the shoulder. He might need a lollypop." She gave him a sarcastic smile, and the non-burned part of her face turned pale. That must have hurt, but at least she was acknowledging him.

Mrs. Young's brow crumpled, and she shook her head. "Well then, I have some burn salve with a bit of something extra in it, and I'm sure I've got bandages somewhere. How bad is the bullet wound?" She turned her attention to Torin.

"It's not bad," Torin said, knowing it had hit nothing major or he'd be bleeding a lot more.

"Right. I'll patch up Miss Reid, then deal with the bullet wound." She left the room, muttering to herself.

Mrs. Young wasn't a mage like most healers. She hadn't done the training, nor passed the tests required to officially become a mage. She was a cook who happened to have healing magic. Though she was from the House of the White Deer, she was unlike most healers in her House and hadn't trained as a doctor or pursued a career in medicine. They were lucky to have her here. Most mages from the House of the White Deer wouldn't dare help the House of Ravens, not while the Deer were so dutifully allied to the House of Owls—the mind mages. Mrs. Young didn't seem to care whom she was allied with. She just wanted to cook and get a big fat paycheck, though Torin secretly suspected she liked it here, bossing everyone around.

"Alright, you lot?" Their classmate Conner sauntered in and grabbed an apple from the large steel fruit bowl on the edge of the bench. He looked up, and when he saw Kira's face, he stopped dead in his tracks. "What happened?"

Kira turned away and looked down with a coy smile. *Was she blushing? Oh, hell no.* Torin was not in the mood for their flirting or idiotic banter. Conner was tall, though not as tall as Torin, but he was bigger and had a face and body that girls seemed to like. Torin couldn't see the appeal himself; Conner had dirty blond hair with too much product in it and a smile that looked fake. He was the bloke who enjoyed flexing his muscles at the gym. Torin had witnessed it too many times for his liking.

"I got hit with a fireball," she said.

Conner whistled. "It got you good. Hope the other guy looks worse."

"Torin got him. He's dead," Kira said proudly.

A hint of guilt prickled the hair down Torin's neck. It didn't feel good to hear that, and he didn't feel the slightest bit pleased about it. "Actually, it was the other guy that hit you. I'm pretty sure he got away."

"He's being modest. Tor used the hand of death on him," Kira said.

Torin wanted to face plant into the table. This was how rumors started. "We aren't sure that's what it was."

Conner held his hands up in fake surrender. "No shaking hands with me then, Mr. Hand of Death," he joked, clearly not believing her. He took another bite of his apple and turned back to Kira. Cocky dickhead.

"I'm fine, too, if you were concerned. I got shot," Torin said dryly, wanting Conner to stop looking at Kira. He found he liked Conner a lot less than he used to recently. They had always been competitive, but it had taken a more serious tone lately.

"You. Out of here now." Mrs. Young came in and waved a tea towel at Conner, swatting him out of the room.

"Come find me later." Conner winked at Kira before giving the finger to Torin. "Good luck with the hand of death thing, mate!" he called as Mrs. Young tut-tutted her way back to her supplies.

Torin didn't have the brain power to respond with a witty comeback. Next time . . .

"Now, let's get you two fixed up." Mrs. Young pulled out a pot of gooey-looking paste and headed for Kira's face. Torin looked away.

Chapter 4

That hour went by too quickly. The wind whistled down the narrow spiral stairs as Torin trudged up, doing his best to ignore the ache in his shoulder—now bullet-free and bandaged up without healing magic. He wished he'd had time to change out of his smoky, blood-soaked clothes, but you didn't keep Korbyn Dumont waiting, and of course, Kira was close behind.

"You don't need to come."

"I do," Kira said in a tone that indicated she may still be a little mad. She was still covered in soot and had twigs sticking out of her hair.

"Your funeral," Torin said, hoping she would take the hint.

"It could just as easily be yours. At least if I'm here, I can go for help if he hurts you."

"Thanks, but don't blame me when you end up with something worse than cleaning duty," Torin said as he glanced back. Her hand moved to her throat, probably without realizing it. He didn't deserve her as a friend.

The breeze buffeting down the stairs grew stronger, and Torin squeezed his eyes against the blast of air. Fortunately, he knew each uneven step instinctively. He was up there several times a week to escape the crowds of the busy house, especially the younger, louder new recruits who liked to run up and down the bedroom hallway in their spare time. Gods only knew why. His quiet time was feeding the ravens, and it was where he usually found Licorice hanging out. Licorice had been his companion and confidant for nearly eight years, and he liked to think of the giant black bird as his familiar, though, according to his father, mages didn't have familiars.

They reached the landing. "Stay out here," he whispered. Thankfully, she nodded and pressed a finger to her lips with a cheeky smile before leaning her head back against the stone wall and closing her eyes.

The ancient hinges groaned with the weight of the door as Torin slipped in and shut it behind him.

"How's the shoulder?" his father asked without turning around.

As if he cared. His father stared out across the fields, scanning the landscape as if an army might pop out at any moment.

"Fine," Torin answered.

"I'm giving you a shot, boy. One shot to prove yourself, and if what Miss Reid claims is true about the sleeping beauty curse or the hand of death—whatever it is—we can go ahead with your apprentice test earlier than planned. The House of Snakes is having an event in two days that will work perfectly with our plan."

By the gods, he actually meant what he said about the test. And so soon? Torin was more than prepared, but this was short notice. "What do you want me to do?" Torin asked; his chest puffed out faking his readiness.

"I want you to show me what you did to that mage. Show me the sleeping beauty curse."

He had to do this, that much was certain. But how the hell was he supposed to demonstrate it? It had been a life-and-death situation, hardly repeatable.

"I'm not sure that's what I did."

"So, Miss Reid was exaggerating, I take it?" His father spun around with a challenging gaze.

"No. I mean . . . I did do something. I don't know what."

"It takes a powerful mind to take control of the subconscious of another—not something I expect you will have. Nevertheless, I have taken this time and deem it is worth the investigation. Do you know how either of the curses works?"

Of course he knew, in theory. But real life was never like the descriptions in the books. Magic was a wild force that needed taming and often took a course of its own.

"Yes, Father. Both work by slowing the heart and forcing the victim into a deep sleep against their will, or in the case of the hand of death, death against their will."

"Correct. Now you will demonstrate it. The House of Snakes draws closer every day; we could use an advantage."

Torin wasn't sure he believed the part about the House of Snakes drawing closer; he had never witnessed any attacks or threats directly from them and thought it may all be in his father's mind. Still, he was certain the House of Snakes had killed his mother, and that was enough reason for now. His father was right about using any advantage.

"Do you remember how you did it?"

"I don't know the power symbol I used. It all happened so fast."

"Excellent, my boy. Even better when it is instinctual magic. This is the symbol you need to focus on." His father went into full teacher mode; he sliced his elemer blade through the air with precision and summoned fine lines of shadows that danced into the room in inky black swirls, not at all affected by the breeze flowing in from the open windows. The lines arranged themselves, floating into a symbol of a triangle made of three spirals, all facing outward, with a crescent moon at the center.

Torin committed it to memory straight away, but it didn't look familiar. His father was watching him closely.

"That wasn't the symbol," Torin said. "It was like a backward 'Z' with its arms curved inward and three bars across the center."

His father's eyes widened just enough for Torin to notice a change. He had to believe him now.

"Come to the window."

Going that close to a glassless window next to his father didn't feel like a good idea. But Torin didn't need telling twice and didn't ask questions. *That* would be idiotic.

"Now summon Licorice."

Torin's stomach dropped to his feet. No. Not his baby bird. She couldn't be dragged into this. He sent a silent prayer to Zakar to send her away, to have some other raven turn up wanting a snack.

"Father, I don't want to try this on her. The spell is dangerous. I could kill her."

"But you were so confident, boy. Don't you want to prove yourself, to become an apprentice?" He did not feign the caring father well.

"I do, but not at the cost of any lives."

"The spell is called *the hand of death*. How were you expecting me to test you?"

"Not with her, please." Torin recognized the desperation in his voice. He was pathetic.

"Perhaps you can't do the spell after all. That's it, isn't it? You and your little girlfriend were lying? I suppose now is the part where you tell me there was no fire mage. It was simply a disgruntled herder?" He took a step closer, but Torin didn't back down.

"It isn't like that, Father." His father didn't even consider his attachment to the bird, he just flipped straight back to lying. This man had serious issues.

Korbyn stormed forward and shoved Torin against the stone wall right next to the window. Below, out of the corner of Torin's eye, the courtyard lurched farther away with the sickening height. He reached for his elemer in his belt, hoping the bastard didn't have the guts to throw him off.

"What was it like? How did you do it? Do tell." A hand shot to his throat, pushing him harder into the coarse stone and crushing his windpipe.

Sweat trickled down the back of Torin's neck as the hand around his throat got tighter. Kira was just outside, but he didn't make a noise to alert her; he had to hope his father would see reason.

"I did it. I'm not lying," he croaked.

"Then why won't you show me? You're nothing but a disappointment." He ground his teeth and shook Torin hard.

Torin gasped in a last breath. He didn't have a choice in this.

"I killed him," Torin wheezed, his lungs screaming for air, blackness creeping into the corners of his vision. "I'll show you . . ."

The hand fell away, and Torin collapsed to the ground, his knees hitting the hard floor with a crack. His lungs spasmed with a cough that wracked his body. *At least I can't feel my shoulder now,* he thought in a strange moment of clarity before he realized what he had just agreed to do.

"Good."

His father yanked him back up, and Torin staggered toward the window. *Please let another bird come. Not Licorice.*

And there it was again. His shoulder was back with screaming pain that shot all the way down his arm. He blanked out his expression, forcing all the pain inside. At this point, showing weakness would only make his father angrier.

"Call to the birds," his father ordered.

Torin looked him in the eye and nodded. The thought of it made him want to vomit. But that was not an option right now. Not unless he wanted to get thrown off the tower.

Torin went to the windowsill and looked straight down to the sloping slate roofs below. He didn't need to call. Licorice croaked from the old weathervane on a nearby roof and launched herself off. Far too quickly, she appeared obediently on the windowsill, her head tilted to the side so she could see out her one good eye. Her other eye was long gone. Torin didn't know how she lost it, but she managed fine with only one.

Her beetle-black eye stared right into Torin's soul as she cocked her head, awaiting treats. He was sorry he didn't have any and suddenly wished none of this was happening. That Licorice would fly away and not come back.

He couldn't do this. He had to save her.

"Get out of here," he used the back of his hand to push her out the window. But she bit the webbing between his thumb, not hard enough to break the skin, but she knew it would hurt him. Stubborn creature. He called out to the other birds, hoping one would come to replace her.

"Enough of this!" His father banged his cane. "I don't have time for this nonsense. Just use this bird." Korbyn summoned a net of shadow and looped it over Licorice without hesitation.

Torin knew what was going to happen next. His hands were shaking. He glanced at the window, hoping another bird would show.

"Is this the symbol you saw?"

A stream of shadow ink crept from his father's elemer once more. The symbol flowed out and twisted into the stark lines that he recognized, the backward Z with bars. Torin's stomach roiled at the sight of it.

Torin nodded. "Yes, that's it. Don't make me do this to Licorice. Let me try the sleeping beauty spell first."

"Very well. The spells are related. Perhaps you only achieved the hand of death because that girl was in danger. It is unlikely you will succeed again. You may try the sleeping spell first."

Thank the gods. Torin moved to the dusty table between two windows, and his father roughly transported the giant black bird from the windowsill through the air.

Sorry you're the guinea pig, Licorice.

Torin stood over the giant bird as she hopped upright. She fluffed her feathers and shuffled her feet expectantly; her face pressed into the net of shadows, confused but staring up at him with all the trust in the world.

Forming a swirling blue spell cloud in his mind, Torin imagined a stoic black raven at the center, just like Licorice. He added the power symbol for the sleeping beauty spell, holding it strong in his thoughts, then slipped his elemer into his hand and cut into the Shadow Dimension to draw the power. His other hand rested on Licorice's silky feathers, cradling her in place beneath the crisscrossing shadows.

Just a little sleep.

He pulled the magic, and it flowed into him like liquid euphoria—pure power. Nothing felt as good as raw magic. Licorice's heart beat steadily beneath his palm, strong at first, but as more magic drew in, it slowed. The thump, thump of her life lulled until there was barely a beat. Her silky feathers grew slick with the sweat from his palm.

That was enough.

He rested her on her side and laid her gently on the table. The faint beat of her pulse was still there.

But before he could withdraw, the spell cloud changed. He couldn't pull his hand away in time.

The triangle spirals warped, the soft lines changing into the harsh lines of a warped backward Z.

No. No! This can't be happening. He willed the symbol to change back, but it wouldn't, and he couldn't pull his hand away. It was as if the magic had a mind of its own.

Then, just like the man, a final thump hit his palm. Horrifying stillness washed over him, and he knew it was over. He yanked his hand away, but it was too late.

"No!" He pressed his ear to Licorice's broad chest.

"You did it, boy!" A firm slap on his back sent a wave of rage rushing through his blood.

"She's dead." A deep well of pain rose in his chest; he wanted to vomit or to punch his father in the face. Neither was an option.

His father spun him around, and Torin was met with a disturbingly gleeful look. Torin's instinct was to bolt for the door. Instead, he set a mask of calm across his face. Now wasn't the time to show his true emotions. He needed to get out of there as fast as possible because there was still a chance he could bring her back. He'd read enough about necromancy; how hard could it be?

"Another one, boy."

Before Torin knew what was happening, his father conjured up a rope of shadows and lassoed two ravens that had appeared on the windowsill and dragged them in, flapping and squawking. The man didn't even notice the birds' distress.

This was the last thing Torin wanted to do. But if this was his one chance to get on his father's good side, he would be a fool to pass it up.

The ravens cawed and protested the tangle of shadows his father forced down on them while he eagerly hovered over Torin's shoulder.

Torin did it again. But this time, he blocked out all emotions.

Two more ravens. Two more last heartbeats.

It was easier not knowing the birds personally, but with each one, a little piece of Torin's soul slipped away. He had never been one of those boys who wanted to kill innocent creatures. He had always liked animals a lot more than people. So much that he wanted to bring them back to life, and for some reason society found that more disturbing than killing.

Yes, that was crazy coming from someone who was training to kill people—or more accurately, one person. But that one worthless bastard who had killed his mother deserved everything that was coming to him. If only the ravens didn't have to pay the price for his training.

"I tried to put them to sleep, but it was like someone else changed the power symbol," Torin said.

"It is the will of the gods—the will of Zakar," his father said as he put his arm around Torin's shoulder. His father was a lot shorter than him, he realized in this bizarre moment. His shoulder was screaming at him, but he clenched his teeth and remained upright. Why would Zakar, the god of dreams, want this for him?

"What I have witnessed here today is a genuine miracle. I am honestly proud to say you possess a rare power—the hand of death," he said in a dramatic, hushed voice.

The hand of death. It sounded ridiculous and seemed highly unlikely; he was sure it was only a myth.

A gasp came from behind him, and both men spun around. Kira stood there, eyes wide, as she looked between Torin and the dead ravens.

"So, it's true then?" Kira said, as she stepped into the room and eased herself closer to Torin.

"Miss Reid. Can't leave my son to do anything on his own."

"He's perfectly capable of doing things on his own. But we watch out for each other."

"That's what you're doing here?" his father mocked.

"Yes." Her eyes locked on Torin's once she saw it was Licorice on the table. She kept her emotions in check, but Torin saw the microsecond of pain flash across her eyes. His throat grew tight.

"With the hand of death comes destruction; that's what the book says," Kira said, almost as if she was thinking aloud, her eyes locked on the dead ravens.

"If you have read your mythology correctly, you will know the hand of death appears when someone has great need of it. Torin is intended for a much greater purpose."

Did he just say that? As misguided as it was, these could be the first words of praise he had ever given.

"Those myths always end in a cataclysmic event," Kira said bluntly, as if only just realizing the seriousness of this *gift*.

Torin was well aware of that fact, and it wasn't something he wanted to think about. Better to focus on the father accepting him part rather than the potentially destroying the world in the future part.

"Don't believe everything you read. We control our own destiny, and the gods have given you a magnificent gift. One I intend to use. Soon, you will infiltrate the House of Snakes and get the justice we deserve."

Torin inhaled sharply. This was it. His chance to do what he was meant to do. A chance for both his parents to find peace. But right now, there was still time to bring Licorice back.

Kira pursed her lips but didn't speak. He knew what she would say, that he needed to practice before jumping into his mission headfirst. He agreed, but not at the cost of more lives.

"I won't let you down, Father."

"You better not. Now take those birds and bury them. A worthy sacrifice."

Not if I have the last say, Torin thought as he dug up all the necromancy info he had collected over the years in his mind.

"Thank you, Father."

Korbyn hit the back of Kira's knees with his cane, and her legs buckled as Torin grabbed her.

"An extra week of morning duty for your insolence," Korbyn said, pointing his bony finger at Kira, and left the room.

Kira shrugged off Torin's hand, and he removed his jacket and laid it out on the table.

"Sorry he made you do that. Poor, sweet Licorice."

"It'll be okay." Torin rushed to bundle Licorice into his jacket, rolling her up like a baby. Kira bundled up the other two birds.

"How will it be okay?" Kira frowned.

"I'm going to bury her," he said, hoping it sounded sincere. Of course, he would do nothing of the sort. But he needed to get back to his room and his books. Perhaps this was what all his secret studies had been leading up to; this was his chance, and he knew Kira wouldn't approve. This was something he had to do alone.

"I'll come with you," Kira said.

"No, you need to rest. Mrs. Young said so. I'll be fine."

Her arms wrapped around him in an unexpected hug.

"You don't deserve this, Tor."

No. Licorice didn't deserve this. He did.

For the briefest moment, he rested his chin on Kira's head and didn't want her to go. At least she wasn't mad at him now.

He stepped back, and guilt threatened to overwhelm him. "Sorry you got hurt."

"It's fine, Torin. I don't blame you. Let's get these birds out of here."

With the birds safely wrapped up, he followed Kira down the stairs, letting her lead until they were back on the main floor where squads of young recruits darted around like panicked ducks dressed in preppy uniforms.

They dodged the crowds until they made it to the stairwell that led down to their rooms. Kira handed him her jacket with the two birds.

"You sure you don't want company burying them?"

He shook his head. What he needed was to get cracking with some illegal necromancy. He hated lying, but this was a good cause. "I'll be fine; go get some rest."

"If you insist. The painkillers Mrs. Young gave me are kicking in anyway. My eyes will hardly stay open. But wake me up if you need me. Promise?"

He nodded. "Will do."

She gave a weak smile, and they parted ways.

But he didn't go outside. Instead, he waited a few minutes, then followed the same stairs down to the bedroom level. As the oldest recruits, their rooms were farther away from the younger kids and closer to the kitchens, though they all connected in a series of cold basement hallways. He checked that Kira's door was closed and darted into his own room across from hers.

Licorice wasn't ready to be a sacrifice.

Chapter 5

T orin bolted the door and walked two steps to place Licorice down on his narrow bed, then unwrapped the singed jacket, spreading it beneath her. He set the other two ravens down near the door.

His room was tiny, more like a prison cell than a bedroom, with white-washed stone walls and basic furniture the same as his squad mates: a single bed, a desk, a set of drawers, and a bookshelf. He'd had a room upstairs like a normal kid before, but when his mother died, he started his training at age ten and moved into the basement barracks with the rest of the recruits. There had been several more in his year at the start; now there were only five, plus between five and fifteen recruits in the other year levels. But they didn't tend to mingle. Discipline was strict, and socializing was not a priority.

At least he had a rug, now. It had taken years to get that privilege, and his red Turkish carpet made his cave-like room a little cozier. He kneeled and fished out a box from under the bed.

His hands were shaking, and he looked down at them as if they weren't his own and wondered why the hell the gods had decided now was the time to reveal this new 'gift,' which certainly seemed more like a curse or punishment.

At the bottom of the cardboard box were the books he'd been hunting for: *Necromancy Through the Ages* and *Necromancy: The Ultimate Guide to Death Magic.* He turned to the page in the latter text with neat yellow sticky notes poking out the top.

He had everything he needed to raise Licorice from the dead. Nodding along as he read, Torin's confidence grew with each page. Studying necromancy had always been a hobby of his—a very secret one, but innocent enough as he'd only ever intended it to be theory. Until now.

Collecting the equipment and ingredients for the spells had been the fun part. He'd never intended to try it in real life; though in his dreams, he had done it many times—simulations where he found his mother and raised her from the dead, and then his father went back to his old self, and then they turned into a magical happy family again. Yes, it was ridiculous. But in your dreams, you could do whatever the hell you liked, and Torin's power over lucid dreams had grown strong and made it all the more real. So real he often confused daylight and reality for dreams.

But he was ninety-seven percent sure this was real, and one hundred percent sure that Licorice hadn't deserved this. Not when she had trusted him to the point of dying. The problem was everyone knew her, and for a raven, she was highly noticeable with her one eye. He would have to smuggle her out and get her as far away as possible once she came back. But how to stop her from returning? That was a problem for future Torin. Right now, he just needed her back.

He stood and rolled up the rug, shoving it in the corner where it crumpled into a pile. Normally, he couldn't handle this level of disorder, but right now, he had more important things to worry about. Reaching across the bed, he cradled her body—so cold and unmoving—and lowered her onto the floor.

"Don't worry, old girl. I'll have you back in no time."

He reached for the large jar of salt that lived on the bookshelf and set out a circle big enough to fit him with his legs crossed and Licorice in front of him.

Sweat poured down his forehead, and his shoulder screamed in pain. The effort from all the magic that day had him shaking and exhausted, but not enough to hit burnout. He could handle one more spell.

With everything laid out in front of him, he cleared his mind of all the clutter, but thoughts of his rapidly changing future charged through at full speed. He pushed them away and focused on the sheen of Licorice's feathers.

He was about to cross a line, but he didn't care. Necromancy might be illegal and from the House of Snakes, their enemies, but resetting the balance in life was far more important.

A knock sounded at the door. Torin twisted to one side to check the bolt—it was locked, thank the gods.

"I'm busy. Come back later," he called, not caring who it was.

"Heard you used the hand of death—for real." Conner. Kira must have messaged him when she got to her room. Hopefully her painkillers had kicked in by now, and she had gone to sleep so she wouldn't hear them and come over.

"Piss off. I'm busy."

"Alright, mate. Was just going to congratulate you. Let me in."

"I'm busy!"

He had to do this now. No distractions. Knowing Conner, he'd get bored and wander off soon enough.

Torin lit the white tea light candle in front of him and set it next to a bowl of water and his succulent plant. He grabbed one of Licorice's tail feathers from his collection on the bookshelf. Pulling one off her now seemed wrong.

Sitting cross-legged on the hard slate flagstones, he cut his palm and dripped the blood onto Licorice—blood magic would enhance the spell. Taking a deep breath, he ignored the pain and cut into the Shadow Dimension. Threads of blue magic traveled through his elemer and into his veins. His head rolled back as he relished the chill of power spreading through him and into the spell cloud forming in his mind, then began chanting under his breath.

"With my voice, I call thee; with my blood, I bind thee; with my power, I draw you forth. My voice shall guide you home. Licorice, I call you forth. By my will, it will be. By my will, it will be. By my will, it will be."

He pushed the magic through his body and back out the elemer toward Licorice. He didn't dare touch her with his hands for fear of killing her again.

Her body twitched, and her head jerked to one side unnaturally.

It's working!

"What are you doing in there?" Conner's voice shattered his spell from the other side of the door.

"I told you to piss off, Conner!" Torin clenched his fists and scrunched his eyes shut as the magic in his blood flared and rippled with anger.

"You're telling me you performed one of the deadliest spells right out of the history books and you don't even want to brag about it? Come on, mate."

The door started shaking, and a stream of shadows crept through the gap near the floor and snaked up the solid wood to the deadbolt and pulled it across. Torin jumped up. This was a classic trick they'd all learned as kids. If Torin had been thinking straight, he would have set a ward up on the door like he did most nights.

Too late now, a flash of movement caught Torin's eye. He froze as Licorice flopped to her other side. *Holy crap, did it work?*

His lungs expanded with a deep, satisfying breath, and he grinned. Distracted by the awesomeness of bringing his dead friend back to life, Torin was too slow to grab the door as Conner forced his way in. Torin lunged, but Conner got his foot in the door.

"What are you hiding?"

"What makes you think I'm hiding something?" Torin put his foot behind the door and held his full weight on it so Conner couldn't get his head in. Torin's eyes flicked to Licorice who was stretching her wings. *Holy shit. I did it.*

"You're only this defensive when you're up to something, Tor. Usually, you just bore me to death with silence or useless history knowledge until I go away."

Dammit, Conner did know him.

The problem was, Conner was bigger and was well practiced in shoulder barging, but Torin saw it coming and braced himself as Conner rammed himself into the door. Ow. Major shoulder pain. Torin winced, and his hand shot to his shoulder as his feet stumbled back, and he crashed onto the bed. Conner stood in the doorway shaking his head.

"Graceful, mate." Then his eyes went as round as a startled toad's and his mouth formed an O shape. "You've got to be kidding me."

Licorice hopped up and staggered around the salt circle. Torin rolled off the bed as gracefully as he could without making his shoulder worse.

"I couldn't let her die."

Conner wasn't as big an idiot as Torin liked to make out; he knew exactly what he was looking at, so there was no point in denying it.

"That's a bloody zombie bird." Conner was looking around, presumably for something to hit her with.

Torin angled himself between his squad mate and Licorice. Conner was right, she didn't look right. Torin's ribs suddenly seemed too tight. The air thinned. This couldn't be happening; he had done everything right.

But there was nothing right about her—or whatever this facsimile of her was. Torin's mouth went dry as sandpaper as he watched in horror. Her wings moved almost robotically, and her head jerked around, her one eye wide in terror.

"Licorice, hey there girl. It's Torin. I've got a treat for you." His voice was too high. Usually, when he told her there were treats, she darted toward him like a hungry miniature dragon. Not this time. The intelligence and understanding were gone; her eye was blank and devoid of life.

"This isn't right," Torin whispered to himself, but he didn't know how to fix it. Panic gripped his chest, forcing air in quick breaths.

"Kill it again or I bloody well will," Conner said, his elemer in front for defense.

Licorice jerked her head and stared right through Torin as if she didn't know him and let out a deep warning croak.

"It's unnatural. Kill it now, Torin." Conner's voice rose.

"No." Torin jumped up and slammed the door shut. Conner backed against the wall. He was usually such a tough guy. If it wasn't so disturbing, it would be funny that he was freaking out over a resurrected bird, but Torin was in the same boat.

A deep croak boomed through the small room as Licorice charged at Conner, wings flapping and talons flailing as she bounced off the desk, then the bookshelf. The broken salt circle did nothing to stop her—he couldn't have used enough blood magic.

The sickening truth clawed into Torin's in-denial brain. He didn't want to face it, but Conner was right.

Please forgive me. He didn't know who the prayer was to, but he had to act now.

Taking in a shaky breath, Torin drew his elemer and summoned a net of fine shadows. It danced through the air and wound its way around the thrashing bird like a living mesh of darkness. Claws and feathers poked through the holes as it closed in, encapsulating and tangling Licorice.

Torin lowered her writhing form onto the ground in a pile of squawking, flapping chaos. His heart clenched as bile rose in the back of his throat. It wasn't meant to be this way. She was meant to survive.

Snake magic is wrong. Necromancy is wrong. Words that had been drilled into him his whole life. But he still wasn't ready to believe it. Even after seeing this. After all, this was his own fault because he'd fucked up the spell, and Licorice was the one to pay the price.

He looked down at the raven that looked like Licorice and knew in his heart she was no longer there. But that didn't mean he was about to give up. He strongly believed that magic between houses should be shared, and this experience was something to learn from. He had to believe it had happened for a reason. After all, wasn't giving life to the dead a better gift than being able to take it away? Didn't it make more sense to celebrate the miracle of resurrection rather than the ability to murder?

The hand of death was looking a lot like a curse now.

"Kill it now, or I will," Conner hissed, his elemer out in front with the blade pointed right at Licorice's chest as he inched closer.

He pulled Conner back behind him. "Get back."

Conner was right, again. There was no way out of it, and this wasn't Licorice anymore.

He crouched down next to the net. "Sorry, girl. I tried, but this is for the best." Torin refused to cry. He hadn't cried since his mother's memorial, and he wasn't going to start now; it would break him.

"Just do it," Conner ordered.

Torin ignored the voice behind him and pressed his hand through the shadow net and rested it on Licorice's still-cold chest. Once more, her heartbeat ticked under his palm, this time erratic and wild. He listened for several seconds as he cradled her tense body.

And all too soon, he blinked it out. This time, it was easy.

"Safe travels to the Shadow Dimension, my friend," he whispered as he lowered his head.

Behind him, Conner let out a loud sigh, and Torin did his best not to spring up and punch him in the face. Instead, he closed his eyes and breathed until the anger passed. His throat was tight as he tried to swallow, and he distracted himself by getting his jacket off the bed and wrapping Licorice up nice and snug.

"Suppose you'll be wanting to be keeping this quiet?" Conner leaned against the door with his arms folded.

Torin raised himself to his feet, face-to-face with Conner, glad to be taller. He could see thoughts ticking over in Conner's mind, deciding whether to rat Torin out or not.

Clenching his fists to his sides, Torin took a breath before speaking. He wasn't about to beg. He had too much pride for that, especially if Conner was going to turn on him anyway.

"You going to continue to be a dick, or are you gonna help me?" Torin said.

"Tell you what. I'll keep my mouth shut if you put in a good word with Mage Dumont once you make apprentice. And hey, I won't even tell Kira if you stop getting in my way with her." He looked Torin up and down in challenge. "Deal?" Conner held out his hand as if this were the end of a rugby match.

Ripples of anger pulsed down Torin's arms. He used every bit of willpower not to punch him. It was fifty-fifty this time. *That prick.* Of course he'd take this as an opportunity for blackmail and to openly admit he was after Kira. It was hard to believe they had been friends once.

"Not a word to anyone," Torin said. He gritted his teeth and squeezed Conner's hand harder than necessary. "And don't forget, I can kill with a simple touch," Torin said before Conner ripped his hand away.

For that second, he'd had Conner's heartbeat in his hand. He knew what he was capable of now, and it terrified him just how easy it would be to kill. His body shook as he kept his emotions at bay; he couldn't let petty anger win. He was better than that.

"Hand of death, remember?" Torin said. He kind of meant it as a joke, but Conner didn't laugh; he narrowed his eyes and didn't say anything further as he left the room.

As the door shut, a wave of reality crashed over Torin. He collapsed onto the bed as a sickening hollowness spread through his chest. Everything had changed.

Chapter 6

The sky was still dark, and the morning air was infused with rosemary as Torin brushed past the overgrown bush by the kitchen door. He was up before dawn, but the entire night had been one gods-forsaken nightmare he couldn't wake up from. Being awake wasn't any improvement.

His throat tightened knowing Licorice wasn't outside waiting to greet him before morning training. Instead, she was wrapped in a tight bundle in his arms.

He moved quickly. When he'd passed through the kitchen, only Mrs. Young and one assistant had started work, and in the distance, the clang of metal told him a few people were up for some early training. Kira would already be down at the training yard cleaning and, no doubt, muttering to herself about it.

But no one was around to give orders at this time of morning. It was peaceful and private as if the only ones on the planet were him, a few rabbits, the deer over the fence, and the ravens . . . all gathered on the eves of the stable across the wide courtyard as if they knew what he had done. Ignoring them, he marched directly to the stable clutching the dead birds to his chest. He grabbed a shovel and set out toward the opposite side of the courtyard, down the stepping stones between the buildings that led to the orchard.

He didn't stop or look back as he marched through the dark silhouettes of stone fruit trees, only stopping when he reached the largest plum tree near the end. Licorice loved this spot; she used to perch there and croak so loud the sound reverberated down the sloping field and freaked out all the rabbits. He was sure she did it for that purpose.

He dropped the shovel and eased his bundle of birds to the ground. Nothing about this was fair. He should have been in control of his magic.

Directing all his anger into his muscles, he plunged the shovel into the damp soil, driving pain into his shoulder with every movement. If his father wasn't so inhumane, he would have found another way to test Torin's new *skill*.

Again and again, with white knuckles, Torin drove the point of the shovel hard into the ground, not stopping until his shoulder was screaming at him and sweat was pouring down his forehead. The soil was mashed up and mangled. He heaved it aside into a rough pile, wanting to scream with every painful scoop of dirt; instead, he bottled it up inside just like he always did.

He wiped the sweat dripping into his eyes with the back of his sleeve. If his father had basic human decency, this wouldn't have happened. If Torin's mother was still around, this would never have happened. Maybe if he had been a better son and done something that day to make her stay, *she* would still be here. The Viper wouldn't have murdered her, and none of this would be happening now.

So much was his fault, but it always came back to the Viper. He had been the one to rip apart their family, and once he was gone, the balance would reset. Torin had known this for years, and his chance was about to come around; he wouldn't screw it up.

Torin straightened up, grabbing his shoulder as a sharp pain shot through it. A misshapen, messy hole in the ground was all he had to show for his efforts.

He crouched down and suddenly found it hard to swallow when he looked at the pile of three ravens.

"I'm sorry. May the goddess Ereshkigal watch over you in the Shadow Dimension, and one day we will meet again," he whispered as he reached over and gently lowered them into the pit.

Across the horizon, the sun painted the edge of the sky a murky red as Torin carved Licorice's name into the tree with the tip of his elemer. Not the correct use for the sacred blade, but right now he couldn't care less.

Near-silent footsteps sounded in the grass behind him. He recognized the pattern in her stride.

"Red sky at night, shepherds' delight." Kira appeared next to him and linked her arm with his.

"Red sky in the morning, shepherds' warning," he said, meeting her eye and regretting it instantly. He loathed the look of pity she gave him.

"You think it's a warning?" she asked. Her face was bandaged, and her lips lacked the tweaked edges of her usual smile.

He frowned. "I don't think we should make assumptions based on unsubstantiated mythology."

"But you know it as well as I do. In *Magic and Mythology* it says—"

"I know what it says, and I know what you're thinking, and no, I don't believe I've got some magical gift from the gods to do something great, and the world isn't going to end in some ridiculous cataclysmic event because of me."

"You don't know that. Not everything can be explained with logic."

"Usually it can be," he said bluntly. "The obvious explanation is some throwback genes are popping up from some ancestor, or I have a weird genetic mutation. Take your pick."

Her arm tensed, and she unlinked it from his. Maybe that was a little defensive. He picked up the spade and started shoveling dirt into the hole.

"Sorry, Kira, I know you mean well. But this is a lot to deal with," he said.

"I just want you to be careful, Tor. You've read more mythology than anyone I know. You know there's always a seed of truth in there somewhere."

He kept shoveling, not wanting to think about this right now.

"Why didn't you bury them yesterday?" she asked.

"Couldn't face it. Why aren't you still cleaning?"

"I got there early and finished early." She let out a quiet sigh. "Sorry about Licorice."

"Thanks," he said.

Scraping the last of the dirt to cover the hole, he patted it down and looked up at the sky as a strip of blue broke through the fading redness. Perhaps a sign that today would be good? He was closer than ever to reaching his goal, and he was certain the Viper would be gone by the end of the week.

The idea of it felt so good he almost smiled, like a weight had shifted.

He turned to Kira. "Remember when Licorice used to wait for you in doorways and drop down and squawk just to freak you out?" Torin said as he nudged her shoulder, trying to show he wasn't grumpy, and held back a wince. "She really hated you, didn't she?"

Kira snorted. "I think she was just jealous of me hanging out with you."

"She *was* the jealous type."

"Fortunately, I have a peace offering." Kira fished something out of her pocket. "I know it was her favorite." Kira placed a piece of fruitcake on the mound of earth.

She always noticed the little things.

"Oi, you two! We've been looking for you everywhere!" A voice racing up the row of fruit trees broke the moment. It was Matt and Dev, the other two members of their squad. The cricket twins, Torin had labeled them in his head when they first met. Both were cricket-mad to a point of obsession, though they looked nothing like twins; Matt was stocky with flat red hair and a splattering of freckles everywhere, while Dev was lean and well-muscled with spiky black hair and brown skin slightly darker than Torin's.

"What's up?" Torin asked as they came to a halt.

"Mission this morning, we need to get cracking. Mage Emerson wants us geared up now," Dev said.

"Mage Dumont put us on the job," Matt said, practically bouncing on the spot.

"This early?" Kira asked.

"They got word the Viper's truck is on the move today. If we leave in an hour, we'll have a chance to intercept it and get a look—we might find the book Mage Dumont is after," Dev said.

Torin shared a look with Kira who was nodding along enthusiastically. Each of them wanted to be the one to find this elusive book. If Torin was the one to find it, he'd be firmly planted on his father's good side.

"Good. This is the chance we've been waiting for. Who's got mission command?" Torin asked, hoping it was him.

Dev looked a little sheepish as he darted his gaze away from Torin. "He chose Conner."

Torin just nodded. *Bloody Conner. Always in the right place at the right time.*

"We better get moving. Meet us in the yard as soon as you've changed," Matt said as he turned and jogged back with Dev.

"Sorry you didn't get command," Kira said. Even with her face half covered in bandages, she looked beautiful.

"Not to worry. I'm sure Conner will do a good job," he said through gritted teeth. He wasn't about to do anything to put this mission in jeopardy, not when it was so important to his father. Plus, he didn't want to give Conner any ammo to spill the beans on Torin's secret necromancy hobby.

An hour later, they were all dressed in casual undercover clothes: Torin in black jeans and a gray hoodie; Kira in blue jeans with a long pink tweed coat; and Conner looked like he was going out on a yacht with white trousers, a blue collared shirt, loafers, and a sweater draped over his shoulders. Dev and Matt wore jeans and England cricket jerseys from some past year. Not the best undercover team.

They stood in line in front of the Rook. The sun had risen above the trees, flooding the stone castle in sharp morning light that made it look almost pleasant.

Korbyn Dumont marched in front of their group. Conner, Torin, Kira, Matt, and Dev stood shoulder to shoulder like the trained idiots they all were, Torin included.

Korbyn tapped his cane on the ground. "In and out as fast as magically possible. Stop the truck, immobilize and disarm the guards, then get to work. The item you seek is a book. It was stolen from me, and we will do anything it takes to get it back. Is that clear?"

"Yes, sir!" they answered in practiced unison.

Finding a book wasn't the most glamorous of missions, but Torin knew how much this book meant to his father. He had to be the one to find it.

"The book is titled *The Shadow Atlas*. It is small, black, and may or may not contain writing. It is a powerful object that must be treated as highly dangerous. If you come across the book, you will not engage with it. You will wrap it in the warded cloth and bring it straight to me."

They remained silent with eyes forward and backs straight.

"You will set the roadblock as discussed and enter the truck via the Hollow. Recruit Conner Stewart is mission commander. Dismissed."

They didn't need telling twice. Conner signaled to them to roll out, and they bundled into the black Lexus SUV with Matt driving and Conner in the passenger's seat. Kira sat between Dev and Torin in the back. It would look suspicious to use the Hollow to get there and set up a roadblock without a car, plus they needed it to carry all their gear.

Torin picked the wrong side of the SUV to get in on. The seatbelt rubbed right across his bullet wound, but at least he was sitting next to Kira, so he felt like he had one up on Conner. It was petty, but he didn't care.

After hours of Conner making them go over the plans, again and again, they finally arrived at the position to set up the roadblock on a wider-than-average stretch of country lane. On either side of them, some black-nosed sheep bleated away. Seeing the sheep brightened Torin's mood a little; they were still fluffy with winter wool, and their silly bleating took his mind off Licorice.

After about half an hour, their target, a generic white lorry, ambled around the bend. The truck stopped where they wanted it to. It was almost too easy. Dev and Matt high-fived each other after subduing the driver and passenger with the last of the starbell toxin. Torin did not envy the unfortunate victims trapped in a very unpleasant temporary paralysis in their seats. At least it worked, and they hadn't had to resort to extreme measures. Torin clenched his fist and held it to his chest. He only wanted to use his power one more time. On the Viper. He was aware and, if he was honest with himself, terrified of how easy it could become. How inhumane he could become . . .

As expected, one of the Viper's men was in the back with all the items. He was the one to worry about.

Conner burst open the roller door as Torin used the Hollow to enter the truck behind the man and sent out a stream of solid shadows to hold his victim down. He was short, stocky, and looked like a fighter. Torin wasted no time and nicked his unfortunate victim with a knife containing the starbell toxin. The man dropped to the ground as his limbs froze up, and his eyes darted wildly from side to side. Torin had a sense the man knew what was happening, but there was nothing he could do.

Torin dragged the stiff body to the edge of the truck where Kira and Matt lowered him out and set him down behind a tree on the side of the road. They'd strategically picked this spot on the quiet country road; it was large enough for a car to pass and easy to hide bodies off to the side.

Conner divided up the work, and they searched the boxes in a grid formation to make sure they got through them all. Most of the boxes contained books, and they were bloody heavy. All they could do was slog their way through and hope no one was tracking the truck.

Thirty minutes went by with no sign of the book. Frustration had Torin throwing books out of boxes as the time pressure weighed down on him. Another fifteen minutes, and they were nearly through all the boxes. But still no *Shadow Atlas*.

A flash of light caught Torin's eye, and a man and a woman appeared in the middle of the road. The man had long hair slicked back in a ponytail, and he wore a three-piece suit with a black detective-type coat. The woman wore knee-high brown boots and a green skater dress with a pale pink denim jacket.

It was clear they were mages from the elemers in their hands and the confident look in their eyes, but they were both too well covered to see their tattoos to know their magic type—a handy thing to see, as mages' tattoos directly reflected their level of power, both changing and expanding as their magic grew. Of course, Torin and his classmates constantly compared tattoos to see who was the most powerful.

His own tattoos had grown nicely over the last few years. The Mark of the Gods, bestowed on him by the god Zakar, was his favorite. It was on his right arm and was a lifelike raven that reminded him of Licorice. The detail in her black metallic feathers was as vivid as real life, and behind her, silvery geometric patterns that shimmered and pulsed were interwoven with metallic stars.

Kira's tattoos were beautiful and contrasted his own. Her raven tattoo was wispy black and gray and had lines like a delicate pencil sketch. Around them were bold red roses that bloomed all the way up her arm.

The man and woman flicked out badges at the same time.

"Paranormal Justice Unit. Just want to ask a few questions," the woman said as they moved toward the truck.

"Move out!" Conner called.

Torin was about to move when the woman conjured a fireball and held it back, hand shaking with tension, ready to throw his way. Torin froze. His vision filled with the memory of the fire mages in the forest. Of the man he had killed.

He didn't even see where his team went. But the screech of tires told him they had left. It was their policy to get yourself out. There was no "no man left behind" mentality around here, and he had been too slow.

Shadow ropes shot out from the man's elemer and pinned Torin against the side of the truck. His elemer clattered to the road. Okay, so this guy was a shadow mage.

"Hello there, love, looks like you're stuck with us. We just want a quick chat," the woman said.

The man snorted. "Fat lot of good that'll do."

"Take no notice of him. He's just grumpy," the woman said. The man shook his head, then turned and looked over the mess they had made in the truck as if it personally offended him.

"I won't help you. I won't say anything," Torin said, just as his father would expect.

Korbyn had told them all about the Paranormal Justice Unit. But Torin was starting to think for himself now. He didn't believe the propaganda his father had done his best to drill into him, that there was no justice in the way they worked, that these were the people who wanted to stamp out magic, hide it from the world, and lock up anyone who was too powerful.

It would be too easy to tell these people everything—they were the law, after all. He could rat his father out, tell them how he and the other recruits had been treated for years, blurt out his concerns about his father's leadership and how he didn't know if what they were doing was right.

And still, he couldn't do it. He couldn't betray his father.

Somewhere deep down, he still loved the man—despite the brutal training, the beatings, and never living up to his expectations, Torin still remembered the man he was before and knew there was still hope. Plus, he had no proof, no evidence that could take him down.

These strangers wouldn't be the ones to take away his chance at making things right.

And so he remained silent as a shadow.

"That's okay. I'll just talk then, shall I? As I said, I'm with the Paranormal Justice Unit. Me and my partner over there are on a special investigations team. My name is Danni Fletcher, and I want to help you."

Chapter 7

Torin had screwed up. He had hesitated, and his split second of weakness had fucked him over. Unforgivable in his father's eyes.

So here he was, muscles straining against the shadowy ropes pinning him to the side of the truck, the bonds growing tighter with each shallow breath, and wondering why this woman wanted to help him. Also, how the hell was he going to get out of this mess?

Right from the start, it was clear this Mage Fletcher woman was playing good cop. But if she was waiting for a response from him, it wasn't coming.

She looked almost bored as Torin refused for the fiftieth time to answer her. Sighing, she tossed a fireball from hand to hand. Eventually, she gave up and peeked around the door to check on her partner.

Torin tried to keep his breathing steady and not panic. But he suspected the bloke in the black coat would play the role of bad cop rather well. The man was in a foul mood. Torin couldn't see inside the truck, but he could hear cursing and boxes crashing.

"At least tell me your name," Mage Fletcher said.

Torin didn't speak. They didn't need to know who he was. He needed to escape, but judging from the tightening bonds, her partner was no ordinary shadow mage. If he could maintain a shadow rope spell this long while doing whatever he was doing in the truck, he was powerful.

The man jumped down from the truck, his black coat flapping behind him. "Nothing's missing. They mustn't've found whatever it was they were looking for."

Good, so they didn't even know they were looking for *The Shadow Atlas*.

"Why did you stop this truck?" Mage Fletcher asked.

Torin stared beyond the woman, down the country road of rolling green hills dotted with fluffy black and white sheep.

Mage Fletcher twisted her mouth in disapproval.

"Let's take him down to the vaults. We can interrogate him later," the man said.

"I think he's a minor. He looks pretty young, and I doubt he'll cooperate if he's like any of the others. How old are you?"

Torin continued to stare past them.

The man turned to him, and something in his expression changed for a microsecond. "You're quite right Danni, he does look rather young. In fact . . ." He looked Torin up and down, then tilted his head to the side and raised an eyebrow. "He fits the age and description of Korbyn Dumont's son perfectly."

Mage Fletcher tilted her head in the same way and twisted her lips to one side. "Could be."

"He looks a lot like Yelena . . ."

Hearing his mother's name threw Torin well off course.

"You knew my mum?" Torin said without thinking. No one ever talked about his mother. Maybe this man could tell him about her . . . And as quickly as that lapse in logical thinking, he had given away his identity. *Bloody idiot.*

The shadow mage pulled a slow smile. "I only met her a few times, but she was a good woman. I'm sorry about what happened to her." His reaction seemed genuine, but Torin narrowed his eyes.

How did he know Mum? Did they work together?

"Are you House of Ravens?" Torin asked, hopeful.

"Nope. House of Snakes." The man rolled up his sleeve and showed a tattoo of a bright silver serpent winding over his forearm. Boiling anger rushed through Torin's veins, and his arms tightened against the shadow ropes, desperate to force his way out. They only grew tighter.

"You dare speak to me about my mother when it was your filthy magic and your House that killed her!" Torin spat, fighting the shadows cutting into his shoulder wound so much he could feel his pulse and the dampness of leaking blood.

The man stepped right up to his face, caught Torin's jaw in his hand, and pressed his thumb into his cheeks as if he were a naughty kid.

"You do not know what you're talking about," he snapped.

Torin thrashed against the bonds. He didn't care who this man was; all Torin knew was he would kill him if he could get his hands free, to hell with his oath from earlier. Killing one more House of Snakes mage wouldn't count.

Mage Fletcher pulled the man back. "Calm down. He's just a boy. It's clear he doesn't have the full story." She pushed the man back, and he threw his hands in the air and stormed off down the road.

"Look, Torin, I believe your name is? I apologize for my partner's behavior, but it's clear you don't have the full story, and I know you aren't going to believe anything we say. So, listen up."

He refused to make eye contact with her.

The woman continued, "We've been tracking your father's actions for some time, and he's becoming more dangerous. A lot of innocent people have died under his orders, and it has to stop."

Possibly true . . .

"You're still young, and I know what you must have been through living under his teachings and following his agenda. But there is another way. If you leave, we can help you. We've done it for others."

That, he wasn't sure about. People had left before, but he had never heard what happened to them. His father led them to believe it was nothing good.

"We can stop the violence and make sure you don't live a life with blood on your hands. You can trust us."

He swallowed. He wanted to trust this woman. Maybe it was the warmth in her eyes or the fact that he was finally being offered a way out. But it wasn't time. He still had a job to do.

"No thank you. I know who to trust," he said coldly. The words tasted bitter on his lips, but he had to make it believable, despite wanting to tell her everything, to yield and give himself over and plead for a fresh start.

"Fine." She held her hands up in surrender. "All I ask is that you think about it. And don't leave it till it's too late. Your father will expect you to kill for him. We have seen it before. You must know deep down this is wrong."

"Thank you for your concern, but I'm good."

She called to her partner, who was checking on the paralyzed guy behind the bush. He glowered at her. "You can release him now," she said.

"You've got to be joking. You're too bloody soft," he called back.

"Nice to meet you, Torin. Here's my number if you ever need help or want a way out." She tucked a card into his hoodie pocket.

Her partner came back over, deep frown lines cutting into his brow. "You sure about this? He could be useful. I bet Korbyn would try to get this one back."

Torin held back a snort of laughter. They did not know who they were dealing with if they thought that was true. His father would sell him to them rather than negotiate on anything.

Still, he had no idea what her angle was here.

The shadow ropes fell away, and Torin slammed into the ground, jarring his shoulder. He sucked in a breath and forced himself up, waiting for an attack. This must be a trick. A practiced play of theirs.

The man stood there with his arms crossed, looking royally pissed off. Mage Fletcher handed Torin back his elemer.

"Remember what I said. Call me if you want a way out."

Torin snatched back his elemer, building defensive spell clouds quickly in his mind in case they attacked. Before they could do anything, he slunk backward and made his way to the front of the truck and cut into the Hollow before they could change their minds. Torin let the darkness swallow him as the gateway closed.

If this guy was House of Snakes, he could easily follow. Torin wasted no time in cutting another doorway out to the forest, about a fifteen-minute run from the Rook. He dropped into a pile of dry leaves and was hit with the familiar scent of damp earth and forest mist.

No time to stop, he set off at a run.

He couldn't cut into the garden Hollow at the Rook in case the Snake mage followed him. If they were being tracked, it was protocol to enter via the warded gates at the edge of the estate, not the Hollow garden within the grounds.

With the chill of spring and nothing but the sound of bird-song and rustling, Torin felt almost himself again as he dodged and wove his way around the secret forest path, a track designed so that anyone familiar could find their way, but enemies would quickly become lost. He knew every twist and turn and boulder and log—all designed to throw strangers off.

The run wasn't long enough as he came to a halt at the black iron gates. Torin rang the bell.

A THUMP hit his back, and he hit the gravel hard. Before he could react, a boot was on his back, pressing him into the sharp, loose rocks.

He glanced up to size up his attacker and recognized the man. "What the fuck, Anders? It's me, Torin," his voice was muffled with his face pressed into the road.

"It's only Torin. Let him up!" someone else yelled.

"Sorry, mate."

Someone pulled him up. Spitting grit from his mouth, Torin dusted off his jeans. His father's men lowered their elemers when they saw it was him.

"What the fuck was that?" Torin asked as he gingerly prodded the bandage under his shirt, now sticky and probably filled with dirt.

"We were told you'd been captured and were expecting Snakes or the PJU to show up at the gates. You escaped, I take it?" Anders said. He was one of Torin's father's most trusted men and usually had better judgment than this; he seemed on edge.

Torin surveyed his father's men as he had seen his father do so often. It worked, as they immediately straightened up.

"Back in positions, you lot," Anders barked at them, and in a swirl of elegant shadows, they dissolved into darkness and slipped back into their ambush spots.

Torin strode with purpose toward the gate, not wanting them to see he was shaken. Anders followed. "Yes, I escaped, but it was only the Paranormal Justice Unit—the PJU. Please let me in."

Though Torin was one of the few who could breach the blood wards of the gates, he felt it was more polite to let the gatekeeper do his job, plus it didn't involve any of his own blood this way.

"Should I call a vehicle?"

"No, I can walk. You better get back to keeping watch. Though, I don't think anyone's coming."

"No worries. Orders are orders. Sorry about the ambush, mate."

Torin just nodded and slipped through the small side gate before breaking into a jog. The long driveway passed by too quickly. He would have liked to have kept running. Instead, he headed for the garden.

Sure enough, a massive team of black-clad soldiers was stationed by the garden gate, and he spotted his own squad amongst them.

Torin's eyes fell on Conner first. He was sweating bullets, and his wide eyes gave away his fear, but his shoulders fell in visible relief when he spotted Torin. Strange, he would have thought Conner would be glad to see the back end of him.

"What happened?" His father was right there, up in his face, nostrils flaring and the vein in his forehead threatening to explode.

"It was the Paranormal Justice Unit, sir. I don't know how they found us," Torin said, quietly catching his breath. Kira's eyes crinkled into a smile, and she gave a subtle thumbs-up at her side.

"How did you get away?" Korbyn asked.

Torin forced himself to meet his father's eyes and felt the eyes of everyone who had gathered around him.

The only way forward was to lie. There was no honor in being set free and no way he was mentioning the conversation he'd had with Mage Fletcher to his father.

"It was luck, sir. I got a hold of my elemer while they were trying to move me and made for the Hollow."

"Luck, my boy?" He looked around, and his gaze fell on Conner, who remained still as a statue. "It wasn't luck. It was the will of the gods. You have been blessed with a gift; it is becoming clear now." Korbyn's hand rested on his cane, and he tapped it with his other hand as if praising himself.

He spun around. "However, I have made a grave error. I clearly overestimated recruit Conner Stewart's competence. As mission leader, he was responsible for his team, and he failed."

Korbyn swung around and belted Conner over the head with the shaft of his cane, fast as a cat in attack mode.

Conner dropped to the ground, stunned. He stumbled up, dazed from the unexpected blow. But Korbyn wasn't done. Torin kept his face blank, but felt for Conner as his father thrust the head of the cane into his squad mate's chest, then kicked out his leg when he tried to stand up. After that blow to the head, Conner went down like a rock, cowering into a silent ball. Korbyn lined up for a kick to the kidneys.

This was their way. In his father's eyes, Conner had fucked up, but Torin couldn't help feeling sorry for him.

"Leave him alone!" Kira yelled.

Don't do it, Kira!

She stepped in front of Conner. His father backhanded her bandaged face without a second thought.

Kira clutched her face and crouched down over Conner, worryingly silent.

"Pathetic! The lot of you," Korbyn spat. He stepped back as if he realized he might have gone a step too far, but didn't acknowledge it. "Get your shit together. None of you deserve to serve the House of Ravens." He spun on his heels and left the garden. Torin assumed his squad had told him they hadn't retrieved *The Shadow Atlas*. At least he didn't have to break that news.

Torin shot Kira a look that he hoped said *are you okay?* She nodded but was biting her lip as she turned back to Conner. Dev and Matt were already helping them both up.

Torin glanced between his father walking away and his squad huddled on the ground. He had to talk to his father now; the others would have to be fine without him. He couldn't lose his shot.

"Father!" Torin ran to catch up with the man, knowing it was a risky time to talk when he was in a mood like this. But right now, Torin was on his good side, and he needed to remain there.

"I'm sorry we failed you, Father. I'd like to make it up to you. We can make up new batches of starbell toxin tonight to replenish our supplies." It was the first thing that popped into his brain.

"At least someone is showing competence."

If Torin hadn't known better, he might have thought his father was relieved to see he hadn't been kidnapped. A comment like that should have resulted in him being called a suck-up. Which he was well aware he was being right now.

"It wasn't their fault I got captured. I was in a dangerous position. It was right for them to leave me there," Torin said, surprised his father wasn't blaming him for all this. The hand of death thing must still have him in the good books at least.

"You all have much to learn. Perhaps I have been too soft."

Soft? Torin nearly scoffed out loud.

His father shook his head and let out a sigh. "Very well. You will make the toxin tonight. Miss Reid will help you. She needs to learn a thing or two about responsibility."

"Yes, Father."

"And tomorrow, have Mrs. Young heal you. I think you've proven yourself tough enough to work through pain."

Was this opposite land? Whatever it was, Torin was going to take advantage of this strange, probably temporary, good side of his father. "Can Kira get healed too? We need her at full strength for training. Our squad is too weak with injured recruits, and we need to be in better shape in case the House of Snakes attacks."

"Very well. Though she hardly deserves it. Off with you now."

Torin stopped as his father marched off. At least that was a win, plus he would have all night to hang out with Kira with no Conner in sight. Things weren't all bad, just mostly bad, but at least he had something to look forward to.

Chapter 8

After a very subdued dinner, Torin and Kira took the darkened stairwell down to the lab in the basement. Torin wrapped his fingers around the cool metal in his pocket, his mother's locket. She had given it to him the last time he saw her when he was ten. She'd said it had secret magic that would guard anyone who wore it. He wasn't sure about that. It had never shown any magical properties, but he wanted to give it to Kira as a peace offering. If anyone needed any extra protection, it was her.

His palms grew sweaty thinking about bringing it up. Not just that, but he wanted to ask her to leave with him again. He had to try to convince her before it was too late.

"Why'd you volunteer us for this again?" Kira asked. She pushed open the stainless-steel door.

"So we wouldn't be tainted with Conner's failures of the day, obviously. Plus, my father gave us permission to get healed. It'll be worth it." Torin put his backpack down on an empty metal bench and pulled out the starbells his father gave back to him at dinner. He was glad the lab was empty.

Kira didn't look pleased. She looked at him like she was trying to work out a puzzle. "What's wrong, Torin?"

"What do you mean? Nothing's wrong. I'm fine." He lied outright. What was wrong was he wanted her to run away with him so they could live happily ever after and she wouldn't turn into a trained killer for his father. Was that so hard to say?

"You killed a man yesterday, you lost Licorice, and you nearly got captured. It's okay to not be okay. Just talk to me."

His eyes blurred slightly as he stared at the wilting starbell flowers. Why was this so hard? He took a breath and faced her, her green eyes pleading for him to be honest.

"I'm going to leave," he said.

"Leave?"

"I've told you before that I want to go. I mean it this time. This place isn't right; my father isn't right."

Her face fell. She wasn't usually one to be speechless, but several long seconds went by before she spoke. All the while, Torin's heart rate kicked up several notches.

"You can't leave, Torin. You're heir to lead the House of Ravens. You're about to get your revenge and make apprentice. It's everything you ever wanted. Why would you throw that away?" Pain and confusion spread across her face—well, the half he could see.

"Kira." He reached out to grab her hand but thought better of it and pulled back. He didn't know how the hand of death worked, but it was definitely triggered by emotions, and he couldn't risk hurting her. "We've all been brainwashed. My father is turning us into soldiers to kill for him in a war we don't even know is real."

"It is real. The House of Snakes . . . they killed your mum for gods' sake! What other evidence do you need?"

"One man. We don't need to punish innocent people for it."

"They're Snakes. They aren't innocent."

"I still plan to take down the Viper. But I won't use my powers to hurt others. Plus, there's no evidence the House of Snakes is plotting against us. They haven't made a move in years, and all we have to go on is my father's word."

"Just because your father and his council don't share things with us doesn't mean it isn't real."

"It doesn't feel right."

"Think about what you're doing, Torin. You would throw everything you have away? And for what? To betray your father to our enemies for some phase or selfish ethical dilemma about killing our enemies? Think for a moment."

He focused hard on the white petals of the starbells as his hands curled into fists. How dare she accuse him of being selfish when all he wanted was to do the right thing?

"I have thought about this for years, Kira. Don't patronize me and call this a phase. You know better than anyone what I have been through. This House is toxic, and it needs to change, but it can't as long as *he* is around."

Kira crossed her arms. "So, what, you're just going to leave me here?"

"No. I want you to come with me."

She paused. It was impossible to read her. "To where? Do you even have a plan?"

Torin allowed himself the tiniest amount of cautious hope. "If my father gives me the go-ahead to take out the Viper, I'll leave after my apprentice ceremony if all goes as planned."

"And go where?"

"Not sure. I'll stay hidden while I gather information, I think."

"You think?"

"Yes." He hadn't planned more than that. All he knew was that once he was out, he would be free to do whatever he liked. As much as it went against his better judgment, he was going to have to wing it on the day.

"Gods, Tor. This is madness."

"Come with me." He reached out and dared to grab her hand this time. "Things will be better; we can do anything we want. We'll get new identities and find out the truth behind everything. I'm not abandoning the House of Ravens. I want to make things better."

She shook her head slowly and met Torin's eye. He knew before she spoke that she wasn't coming. Her hand dropped from his.

"I know you mean well. But I can't just leave, Tor. I'm sorry. My family sent me here with expectations. I've trained for six years to get to this point, and I could be next to make apprentice. I can't do that to them."

His fingers curled into a fist which he pressed hard into the table as if the cold metal could draw out his anger. "I don't want to leave you here. It isn't safe."

"I'm not asking for your protection. I'm a big girl and I can look after myself."

He let out a slow breath. She did need him. She didn't know how many times she had been *that* close to tipping his father over the edge. If he hadn't been around watching out for her all these years, she'd be expelled by now. Or dead.

He turned away from her and started setting up the distillation equipment, focusing extremely hard on the glassware in front of him. There would be no convincing her; he saw it in her eyes, that stubbornness, the loyalty to her family. Even if—in some crazy scenario—she was in love with him, she still wouldn't leave.

"I can do this alone. Maybe you should go get some rest," he said through gritted teeth. He nodded to the starbells in front of him, but she knew what he meant.

"Fine. I don't want to be around you when you're talking this nonsense, anyway."

"It isn't nonsense. I'm serious."

"You can't be. The Torin I know would never abandon his responsibilities and his family like this."

"Maybe you don't know me as well as you thought."

Her eyes grew fiery. "Maybe I don't. But if you leave, just know I will never talk to you again."

She flicked her braid over her shoulder and stormed out. It was clear she didn't believe him still; she wouldn't have given up that easily if she did.

He shoved his hand in his pocket, and the cold metal of the locket bit into his palm.

So, that didn't go so well . . .

He sat there staring at the measly bag of starbells. The lab was too cold, and the blue light filtering from the fridges and various buttons made for a gloomy atmosphere and what was sure to be a long night of making starbell toxin alone. The regret of volunteering was real, but perhaps claiming a wee bit of starbell toxin for himself would make it worthwhile.

It was only 8 a.m., and Torin was covered in sweat and mud from training, already wanting to crawl back into bed. He was drained from lack of sleep, stress, and pushing his magic hard; he had no idea what day it was anymore. He hadn't had time to go get his shoulder healed.

But Mage Emerson waited for no one, and after a two-minute shower where he got his bandage soaked, he hastily slapped on a new wound dressing and changed into his day uniform—the same black trousers, white-collared shirt, black and silver striped tie, and fitted blazer he'd worn nearly every day for the last six years—and left his room.

His shoulder was giving him grief. Maybe he could get permission to skip the start of class to get it healed. He wouldn't hold out hope.

None of his squad mates were in the hallway, just a few third-year kids testing the limits of being late to class. He set off alone toward the classroom on the other side of the castle. It was just as well because he wasn't in the mood to talk to anyone.

Ten minutes later, Torin was on the other side of the Rook doing his best to ignore the pain in his shoulder as he stepped into the familiar dingy classroom. The room was on an angle that didn't receive sunlight at any time of day. His father most likely chose it for that reason; it was depressing.

The classroom comprised twenty desks, but they only filled five. There had been more students in the beginning. They were gone now, either killed in training or banished. Torin tried not to think about them anymore.

"Your face looks much better," Conner said, smiling at Kira who settled into the desk between him and Matt. Torin blanked his expression so it wasn't obvious how bothered he was by Conner. But he was right about her face; it had been healed with magic, leaving her skin with a rosy tinge to it and as smooth as a starbell petal. She must have gone to see Mrs. Young last night, and he was wishing he had done the same, but it had been too late by the time he had finished up.

Torin slid into the desk behind Conner so he didn't have to look at his face. The guy was grating on his nerves, being all upbeat and pretending like yesterday's failure had never happened. Dev dashed in after Torin with a panicked look in his eyes.

"Heads up, lads," he hissed as he crashed into his seat beside Torin.

Torin swiveled around to see what he was referring to, and his veins turned to ice when his father walked into the training room. This was not good. His father never came to their classes, and there was no way he could skip out now.

Conner, Kira, and Matt stopped chatting and sat bolt upright, eyes toward the front when they heard his voice.

"Good morning, class." Korbyn Dumont walked up the center aisle, tapping his cane in a slow rhythm while grinning like a maniac.

"You must be wondering why I have decided to grace you with my presence today?" He spun around when he reached the front, like a deranged circus master holding his cane in the air. He did things like that because it made people uncomfortable—throwing them off guard straight away was one of his weird power moves.

Everyone sat in silence. Torin's shoulder throbbed beneath his fitted blazer, but he knew better than to move.

"The answer, my dears, is that I had a revelation today. Thanks to my son, I realized I have missed a key lesson in your education, and today we shall remedy that."

His father's eyes locked onto his, but he remained still and calm. *Don't let him see your fear.* Torin wondered which part of his fuck-up his father would focus on today.

"Today we will learn the sleeping beauty curse, also known as the sleeping beauty spell."

It was as if the air had been sucked out of the room.

His father continued. "A rare and difficult piece of magic, but one my offspring has mastered an advanced variation of when facing an enemy in the field."

Great, just what he needed.

"It requires great focus as you take control of the subconscious mind in order to slow the heart and force the victim into a deep sleep. On the off chance any of you can master this useful skill, we will be attempting it today. As the House of Snakes draws in closer, we need every advantage we can get," his father said.

A group of white rabbits appeared on the table at the front of the room, having no doubt been concealed by a cloaking spell for dramatic effect.

Mage Dumont waved his hand above them, and one by one, they fell asleep.

Matt gasped. "They aren't dead, are they?"

Kira stood up at her desk, craning her neck to get a look. Conner pulled at her blazer, frowning at her to sit down.

"No, they are not dead. I'm sure they're thankful for your concern. It is only a very rare magic that can stop the heart. Most of us only have the gift to slow it. Usually, it is too much to convince a mind to overpower itself enough to stop a heart completely."

The blood drained from Torin's face as his father's eyes settled on him. He was setting Torin up for a demonstration. His squad mates had all heard the rumors by now, but it wasn't exactly something he wanted to practice in front of people.

Mage Emerson entered the room and eyed the sleeping rabbits as she made her way to the front. Torin relaxed a little. At least if she was there, things wouldn't get out of control with his father, who sometimes liked to push a little too far.

Mage Kat Emerson wasn't soft; in fact, she was the opposite—terrifying. She had been their trainer since they were twelve and had been Torin's father's top assassin for years before that. Her sleek, jet-black hair was, as usual, tied in a high ponytail, and her skintight black outfits left nothing to the imagination.

"This spell can only be used in direct contact with an enemy. The hardest part is getting close to them. When it is unnecessary to kill, this is a useful spell to have up your sleeve." Mage Emerson explained to the class the theory of how the spell should work and demonstrated once more as Mage Dumont nodded along.

One by one, his classmates were called to the front to attempt the spell on a poor unwitting rabbit. None of them made them sleep with their first attempts. Not surprising, as it was well above their level of learning. Their training was more in combat magic using shadows and a little in dream manipulation once a person was already—asleep—nothing like this.

Of course, Torin was last to be called.

"Your turn, boy," his father said.

Torin wiped his hands on his trousers and made his way to the front with his elemer tightly in his grasp. He shot a look to Mage Emerson, wishing she would intervene, but knew she couldn't, not with his father there.

Torin didn't want to kill the rabbits. Making them sleep would be a far more useful skill. But he was terrified of his lack of control. He was used to mastering spells and having them behave as he wanted. This one was unpredictable and dangerous, but he could beat it.

He stood over the rabbit as it shuffled around on the desk. Its black eyes looked up at him as its nose twitched and its little whiskers flicked side to side. He could do this. *Just focus on the power symbols for the sleeping beauty curse.*

He formed a swirling blue spell cloud in his mind with the raven at the center. He added a power symbol for sleep and the sleeping beauty curse, holding it strong in his thoughts. In one hand, he held his elemer, and with the blade, he made a small cut into the Shadow Dimension to draw power; his other hand rested on the downy soft back of the rabbit, cradling it in place.

Just a little sleep.

He pulled the magic through and relished the way it spread through his veins. The rabbit's heart beat steady beneath his palm. He focused, and as more magic drew in, it slowed and slowed until there was barely a thump. Its fur clumped with the sweat from his hand.

He was doing it.

But something changed. He knew what was about to happen, and he couldn't stop it. It built in him like an inferno of flames, the magic so strong it overrode his will, wanting to fulfill its purpose.

It was the same as the man in the forest, the same as Licorice. There was the inevitable final thump, then a surge of stillness washed over him.

Not again.

"He's done it!" his father slapped him on the back. Torin tried not to hurl from the jolt to the unhealed bullet wound. His father's unsettling grinning had Torin wanting to run from the room.

"It's dead, not asleep," Torin said. He didn't dare look at Kira.

"He's right, it is dead." Mage Emerson confirmed with her brows knitted together. Torin's father picked up the rabbit as if it were a trophy.

"Wonderful," Mage Dumont said, still grinning.

Torin's squad mates watched silently, but their reactions gave away their awe: Matt sat there slack-jawed; Dev was beaming with wide eyes, clearly impressed; Kira leaned in like she was studying the rabbits, though her eyes flicked to Torin as if trying to work out what he was thinking; and Conner leaned back in his chair, glaring at Torin in warning. It was like he wanted Torin to slip up so he could spill the beans on the necromancy thing.

"Try another one," his father ordered.

That was the last thing Torin wanted to do.

Two more rabbits. And like the ravens, two more pinched-out lives.

With each one, the hauntingly familiar pieces of his soul slipped away. He hated himself for killing these innocent creatures. He wasn't cut out for this.

The class sat in silence as Torin's father urged him to kill every rabbit. Each time, he tried his best to put them to sleep, but the power symbol always turned from a triangle to the backward Z.

"They're all dead, Father," Torin said, as bile rose in the back of his throat.

His father patted him awkwardly on the shoulder.

"What you have witnessed here today is a true miracle of the gods." He paused for dramatic effect and to make sure all eyes were on him, which of course they were. "I am proud to say that Torin possesses a rare power—the hand of death."

It was clear they had all come to the same conclusion. His father just had a flare for the dramatic. The room remained silent, but inside, a symphony of tension was vibrating every one of Torin's nerves.

His father continued. "Torin will be the first of you to undergo his apprentice test, and it is happening tonight."

Torin's chest tightened. *Tonight?* His father had never actually confirmed they were doing this, but apparently they were. How had he let time slip away from him so fast? He was nowhere near prepared for the most important mission of his life. But at least he had the killing part down.

His father removed his arm from Torin's shoulder and continued as if he hadn't just dropped that bombshell. "As for the rest of you," he pointed his cane around the room, "I expect you to master the sleeping beauty curse or you're out. We have more rabbits coming. You will remain here until you succeed."

He turned to Torin. "I suggest you get some practice in before tonight, Torin, though you don't appear to need it. You know the plans; you can use your new gift to make this mission even more efficient. A nice clean job."

Torin's stomach dropped. He knew the plans for the mission back to front. They'd been going over them for months in preparation for this day: plant the bugs for the monitoring of the House of Snakes council, look for *The Shadow Atlas*, wait for the Viper, then take him out before the council joined him for their scheduled meeting. Quiet and unseen was the key. The hand of death could make this a lot quieter and a lot less messy. All he had to do was ensure he could get close enough to the Viper to use it.

This particular scenario was developed to be carried out during a House of Snakes council meeting. According to intel from his father's spies, the Viper, Head of the House of Snakes, was predictable in his routine before meetings. A fact they were counting on.

But on no sleep and little practice at this new skill, Torin wasn't exactly confident he could pull this off. But to look on the bright side, he had the rest of the day to prepare and pack to leave for good.

Chapter 9

A brand-new suit was hanging on Torin's door when he arrived back at his room after an afternoon of intense training and an even more intense healing session with Mrs. Young. The suit was a reminder of what tonight would be, a deadly mission plus a party.

Torin had dosed up on supplements to take the edge off the healing, and wanted nothing more than to flop down on his bed and go to sleep, but he no longer had the luxury of time. There was only an hour and a half until he had to leave with his father. It didn't seem real.

Pacing the tiny room, he grew more and more agitated with every step. Not only was he going to avenge his mother's death tonight, but he would also make apprentice status and run away from home. He had the urge to laugh out loud at the ridiculousness of it, but he held it in and thought about what he should pack.

His eyes kept falling to the card on his desk: *Danni Fletcher, Senior Agent, Paranormal Justice Unit*. It sat there, glowing white in the dull light. He picked it up. Her office was beneath the London Silver Vaults.

He wouldn't resort to drastic actions with the PJU this early on; he needed proof of something against his father before that.

Or maybe he wouldn't find anything and prove himself wrong about how bad his father was. It would almost be a relief if that were the case. He might be exiled, but at least his father wouldn't be the crazy one.

Either way, he had to know. He was doing it and leaving tonight. End of discussion.

He pulled out his black backpack and threw it on the bed, still singed and smelling of smoke. But what to pack?

His eyes trailed over the items he had used in the ritual for Licorice, all lying on the floor where he'd left them; a tipped-over bowl, the feather, salt, and dirt were scattered across the stone floor. He hadn't even bothered to put the rug back. No point now.

He gathered everything he cared about in a pile on his bed. It wasn't much: the *Magic and Mythology* book he and Kira had read countless times, his two necromancy books, his three favorite pens, two notebooks, Licorice's feathers he'd collected, a few pairs of underwear, socks, and a spare shirt.

He wouldn't need his day uniform or training uniform where he was going—wherever that was. He spotted the vial of starbell toxin and tucked it into the front pocket of his bag and shoved everything else in the top.

Last of all, he took his mother's locket and draped it around his neck.

Right, that was done. He couldn't afford to waste any magic with extra training right now. He would need to be in top shape for later tonight. Reading was the only thing he could think to do to stop talking himself out of his own crazy plans, but first, he needed to get dressed for his big night.

He took the new suit out of its bag. Not exactly what he wanted to wear, but Mr. Sampson was good at picking things that suited Torin. The dark blue trousers he pulled on were well-fitting. He adjusted himself and looked in the mirror before deciding they looked okay. He would have preferred a black shirt but put on the white dinner shirt, then slipped on the dark blue dinner jacket and tucked the House of Ravens cufflinks into his pocket. He turned in front of the mirror. It would do. He took off the jacket and hung it by the door, all ready to go.

Necromancy: The Ultimate Guide to Death Magic peeked out of his bag—perhaps a bit of light reading to keep him occupied for the next eighty minutes? He had been meaning to read up on what might have gone wrong with Licorice, not that he ever wanted to go through that again.

He settled into his reading zone on his bed.

A quiet knock broke Torin from his concentration. He had been reading about zircons grounding a body to this plane. He checked his watch; only ten minutes had gone by.

"Tor, are you in there?" Kira's voice was faint outside the door.

He instantly straightened up. This was his chance to make up with her before he left. He had to make it right.

"Come in," he called, hating that his voice gave away his nerves.

The door opened a crack, and Kira slid through. She was still dressed in her uniform blazer and long black skirt, but her hair was now in French braids on either side of her head.

"Um, hey. Happy birthday, Tor," she said and tossed him a bag of wine gum sweets.

"Thanks . . . It's my birthday?" The words stumbled out of his mouth as he turned the wine gums over, not comprehending what she had just said. How could he forget his own birthday?

He shifted the book under his leg, hoping Kira hadn't noticed it, as he pushed himself up against the white-washed wall.

"Yes, and now I feel awful. I'm sorry we fought and that I'm such a terrible friend and that it took me all day to talk to you. I was just so angry. I ruined your birthday. Please forgive me," she rambled, her hands clasped together in front of her.

"Of course I forgive you," he answered automatically. It was all his fault, anyway. "These came from your stash under your bed, didn't they?" he said, holding up the bag of sweets.

"Course they did." She threw herself on him in a big hug, and he automatically wrapped his arms around her in response. He tensed. She was probably wondering if he was leaving—that was why she was here.

If she hadn't believed him before, maybe she would now. Now that he knew it was real.

Her face pressed into his chest, and he could feel her breath on his collarbone. Suddenly conscious of his own chest rising and falling so closely against her, he wanted to kiss her, but he wouldn't. He wouldn't risk his last memory being a slap in the face.

"I'm sorry, Tor."

"You already said that." He rested his chin on top of her head. She didn't seem to want to move away; her arms around his middle grew tighter.

She let out a quiet sigh.

"I should be the one apologizing to you. I acted like a complete wanker last night, and I didn't even know it was my birthday, so you can't feel bad about that."

Birthdays were never important to him, though this one should have been one he remembered: the big sixteen. He felt her chuckle, and she slowly pulled away to sit up and look at him. Her face fell into seriousness.

"So, you're going to do it then?" Kira said.

"I've been training for years for this. Of course, I'm going to do it."

"I didn't mean *that*. I meant, you're going to leave. Aren't you?" Her voice quavered at the end, and she pulled her knees to her chest.

He nodded. Unsure what to say, he glanced at his bag by the door, and she noticed.

"You're already packed?" She took in a sharp breath.

He nodded. "Yup." What else could he say?

"I didn't think you would actually go."

"I tried to tell you. But I have to. I can't stay here. The offer still stands, you know. You can always come with me," he added hopefully.

"I want to . . ." She snuggled in next to him so they both leaned against the cold wall. Her head rested on his shoulder. "But I can't. You know that."

He nodded. She would never turn on her family like that. Somehow that made it easier for him, having a father who was so easy to hate. He couldn't deny that he loved him too, deep down, but it wasn't the same as having people who would genuinely miss you. His father would disown him before he admitted he cared for him. Maybe Kira would be safer here than on the run. He liked to hope so.

Kira looped her arm into his as if that would keep him there, anchored down. "You're not going to turn on us, are you? You're not going to the Paranormal Justice Unit?"

She looked up at him, and he shook his head. "No. I need to find out the truth first. See things from the other side. I want to find out what he's hiding, what he's actually done, and I can't make decisions when I'm blind to all the facts. So, I'm going to disappear and find out as much as I can before I act on anything."

"Good." She nodded to herself. "But where will you go? How will you survive?"

"I've been taking cash out of my bank account for years; I've got enough to survive. I plan to get a fake identity, and I'll work the rest out as I go. I'll be fine, Kira."

As if on cue, thunder rolled through the skies overhead before cracking, and even through the thick castle walls, the sound of heavy rain crashed down. Torin could imagine it blanketing the green hills in cascades of icy water.

Kira flinched at the lightning crack.

"I'll take that as a good omen," Torin said.

"How very un-Torin-like. But I should like to think so as well, being a supportive friend and all."

"Thanks, I need all the support I can get. I suspect there won't be much of it after today."

"The life of an outlaw . . . It almost sounds appealing. It's kind of romantic, don't you think?" she said.

"I think you've been reading too many books."

She freed her arm and hit him in the shoulder. "Too many books, what a hypocrite. Speaking of books, what's that you're reading?"

She grabbed the book out from under Torin's legs before he had a chance to stop her.

"Give it back," he said, trying to yank the book from her hands, but she had an iron grip on it.

"You're not hiding porn in here, are you? You know you can get that on the computer, right?" she joked as she flicked through the pages, then stopped and froze on a page before slamming the book shut and studying the cover. Her eyes rose slowly with a glare that would cut laser holes through Torin's face if she could.

"Give it back. I can explain."

"What the hell, Torin? *Necromancy Through the Ages*. Are you fucking serious?"

"It's nothing, just a silly book. Give it here."

She exhaled through her nose. "It's illegal just reading a book like this. Don't tell me you're thinking of trying it. This is dark, even for you, not to mention magic from the House of Snakes—our enemies, if you hadn't forgotten."

"Keep your voice down," he hissed.

"What were you planning on doing? Bringing those rabbits back to life? Licorice? People?"

"Course not. I was studying, that's all." *And maybe I was thinking about bringing the rabbits back to life.*

She shuffled away from him slightly, causing anger to spark through him. If anything, she should fear the hand of death, not the magic that reversed it. This is what was wrong with the world. If his father had bothered to learn this sort of magic, maybe Torin's mother would still be around. How was this a bad thing?

"It's dark magic. You need to be careful, especially if you're out there without backup."

He took in a controlled breath, but the heat in his blood was climbing fast.

"How could this be dark magic if I'm bringing back what I took from them? How is that wrong?"

She folded her arms. "It just is."

"I don't want to argue with you again."

"Good. I don't either, but I'm starting to question your judgment. I think it's wrong to leave."

Back to this again. The truth of what she thought. He took the book from her and shoved it into his bag.

"You can't talk me out of it. Maybe you should just go. I need to meet my father soon, and I should get ready." His voice was cold. It was better if she left now, even if she was pissed off at him, before he said something he would regret and left her hating him forever.

"Just stay," she said so quietly he almost didn't hear her.

He shook his head slowly. He had to do this, had to do what was right. She would understand later.

"I can't," he whispered as lightning crackled overhead. Kira flinched.

She hugged herself, looking small and sad. He'd never seen her like this. Vulnerable.

"I like you, Torin. You're my best friend, and all you had to do was ask me out. But you never did. I can't believe Conner was right about you." She wiped her cheek and refused to look at him.

She liked him? Or *had* liked him . . . until now. He was an idiot. What had Conner told her?

"Right about me how? What did Conner say?" His mind latched on to that detail and blocked out the rest.

She stood and marched toward the door before stopping and turning back. "So, it's true then?"

"What?" Torin snapped, suddenly feeling like everyone was against him.

She rubbed a hand across her forehead, squeezing her eyes shut. "I went mental at him because I was so sure he was lying when he told me about Licorice." She looked up and shook her head. "I was so sure he was trying to drag your name through the mud just to get in my pants. But he was right." She let out a humorless laugh.

Torin scrambled. "He is trying to make me look bad, Kiri. And he *is* trying to get into your pants."

Why do I say stupid shit without thinking? He needed to stay calm; it wasn't an option to get angry.

She put up her hands. "Oh, okay. So, you haven't been doing illegal necromancy?"

Blood pounded in his ears. *Fucking Conner.* He was so worried about Conner going to his father, he hadn't thought he'd play it this way. He wanted to make sure Kira hated him as well. It seemed to have worked.

He took a deep breath. "It was Licorice. You have to understand—"

"I understand enough. Goodbye, Torin. I hope you have a nice life screwing us all over."

She was leaving, and he didn't know what to say to make it right.

"Please, Kira. Don't go. Calm down. I didn't mean for any of this to happen. Just let me explain."

She reached for the door, and his heart sank. She couldn't leave now. Not like this. She turned back, just for a second and that was all he needed. He stepped toward her and lifted her hand from the door.

"I couldn't let Licorice's life be wasted like that. I owed it to her; can't you see I was trying to do the right thing? I don't want you to hate me, Kira."

Her pulse raced beneath his palm as he pulled her toward him.

Her hand folded into his so naturally, and she stood in front of him biting her lip. The thump, thump of her heart slowed in his palm, and he realized he was controlling it. His own heart rate slowed, matching hers, and gradually her anger trickled away.

He was doing it, controlling his "gift."

"I could never hate you, Torin. You have a good heart, and I'm sorry I lost it, but this is too much." She squeezed his hand.

He wanted to reach down and kiss her, to feel her soft lips against his, to tell her he wanted to be with her, even if it was only once—even if it was only a fantasy.

Before he could do anything, symbols flashed across his vision, and her heartbeat grew so loud he was sure he could hear it in his own ears. His grip tightened around her hand, and his stomach plummeted to his feet when he realized what was happening.

For a frozen second, their eyes locked. She could feel it too, that he was losing control. She tried to pull away, but he was too strong. The magic was too strong.

Before he could do anything, magic pulsed through him, fueled by confusion and amplified emotions. The dark magic spiraled up, and he couldn't let go.

"What's happening?" she cried out as his grip on her hand grew tighter.

The thump-thump of her rising heartbeat spread from his hand and up his arms. Before he could rein it in, the drumming was suppressed.

He tried to fight it, but the spell cloud formed in his head without him telling it to. Time stood still as he fought with his mind, and he did everything he could think of to retract the magic.

But the pull was too strong.

She blinked slowly, her eyelids staying closed longer each time. Stumbling, he lowered them both to the bed and gripped her chin with his free hand.

"Kira, stay with me," he said, shaking her.

This was not happening. He could control this.

But her eyes remained shut, and his nightmare became true as his hand stole away her last heartbeat.

She collapsed into his arms, and her hand dropped from his.

"No, no, no! Kira. Kira! Wake up."

She couldn't be gone. She couldn't be dead.

He shook her body like a heavy puppet as he pulled her onto his lap. Her eyes were blank and stared up to nowhere. Icy panic rushed through his veins, twisting with frigid fingers around his pounding heart.

This couldn't be real.

"You can't be dead," he whispered.

His shaking fingers grazed her neck. It scared him to touch her bare skin, but he pressed into the point where there should be a pulse, hoping desperately for that tiny thud of life against his fingers.

There was nothing.

The sting of tears blinded him, and he twisted around, searching for something to make this better, something to tell him it wasn't real.

There had to be something he could do. *Think. Think. Think, Torin*! His breath was shallow, and her body was growing heavier in his lap.

Necromancy.

His eyes fell to his bag and the necromancy book sticking out. He knew what he had to do.

"Come on, Kiri. I'll bring you over here, and we can make things right," he said as desperation crawled across him like a parasite.

He lowered her to the stone floor, trying to drown out the panic that was quickly rising, not caring if she never talked to him again, she just had to come back.

Stumbling up, he grabbed the salt from the shelf, then pulled in the items scattered across the floor with shaking hands. He set the candle, bowls, and feather next to her and made a circle around her, forming his spell cloud as he went.

The candle wouldn't light, and dizziness tugged at him, threatening unconsciousness from overusing his magic. The uncontrollable shaking in his hands only added to his panic.

Opening the pouch of gemstones from the front pocket of his bag, he shook out the contents, desperately searching for zircons. He found two, which would have to do, and he placed them on Kira's stomach and cut a gash in his hand with his elemer, not even registering the pain as he wiped it across her forehead and the top of her chest.

"Sorry," he whispered as he lifted her shirt and put a hand-print of blood on her stomach. Blood would strengthen the spell if it was directly on the body.

Calming his mind was the hard part. With extreme force of will, he separated the screaming part of his brain from the logical part while adding all the necromancy symbols he had ever learned to his spell cloud.

Forcing the good memories to bubble to the surface, he focused on all the positive things he could think about Kira: her smile first thing in the morning at training, the way she bounced up every time she was knocked down, the way she teased him for not letting his food touch on his plate, the way she ate every disgusting tomato he found in his food, her laugh . . .

He *would* bring her back. If anyone deserved to live, it was her.

Chanting against the background noise of thundering rain, he called to her spirit and to the gods to restore her to her body.

"With my voice, I call thee; with my blood, I bind thee; with my power, I draw you forth. My voice shall guide you home. Kira Reid, I call you forth. By my will, it will be. By my will, it will be. By my will, it will be."

Minutes ticked by as he sat there chanting, praying, drawing in streams of magic until his back was stiff and aching.

When he came out of the trance, a wave of nausea rushed over him, and he nearly threw up.

Please be okay, he prayed as he leaned over her, shaking fingers resting on her neck. Her eyes were closed.

A jolt of hope shot through him. He held his breath, and a pulse thumped faintly beneath his fingers.

Thank the gods. Thank Zakar, thank Gula, even Ereshkigal who served the House of Snakes.

"Kira. Kira!" Relief washed over him at the faint pulse, but she didn't wake up.

No time to waste. Her spirit might have returned, but she still needed urgent medical attention. Mrs. Young would know what to do.

Torin stumbled up.

"Come on, Kira. Stay with me, just a bit longer."

He scooped her up in his arms and raced across to the kitchen, thankfully not passing anyone on the way.

Mrs. Young and Mr. Sampson, the butler, raced in and glanced between Torin and Kira. He must have looked crazed and was possibly covered in blood. He had no idea.

"Help her," Torin croaked. "I'm fine." Shutting his eyes, he leaned against the cupboards as a wave of dizziness came over him.

The ticking of a wall clock drilled into his brain as Torin awoke to find himself on the yellow sofa in Mr. Sampson's room. The worn floral cushions and the painting of willow trees by a tranquil stream were familiar and strangely comforting. He'd enjoyed sitting in here as a boy while Mr. Sampson polished silver and watched football.

Mr. Sampson was at his side. "Torin. Can you hear me?"

Torin nodded. His mouth was tacky and dry. "Kira?"

"You were out for a minute there, lad. She's with Mrs. Young now. She seemed to think the young lass had had a heart attack. Strange thing. She hasn't woken up yet."

"I need to see her." Torin sat up. *He had fainted? At a time like this? Pathetic.*

"Later. You need to be on your way. Your father'll be looking for you."

"Shit." Torin glanced at the clock and found it was already a quarter past five. He needed to leave in fifteen minutes. This was a day he'd imagined for years, and this sure as hell wasn't how it was supposed to go.

"You don't have to do this," Sampson said, quite out of character.

Torin studied the man's face. He was serious.

"I need to."

"Things aren't always as black and white as they may seem. I've heard things, you know. Things from the day your mum passed."

"What things?" He needed to see Kira so he could get moving, but for this, he would risk being late.

"No one saw your mum that day. Your father stormed off in an almighty rage, and when he returned, he told us your mum was gone. That's all there was to it."

"Why didn't he bring her back?" Torin knew nothing of that day. His father refused to speak of it.

"They say the Viper came out of the Hollow carrying her body, but there was no proof of murder. They put it down as suicide. Death by her own elemer." Mr. Sampson's eyes filmed over. "She was a lovely lass, your mum."

Suicide? No one had ever mentioned that. No one ever mentioned anything to do with his mother; it was an unspoken rule around here. But that would be why the Viper was never accused, how he had gotten away with it. Torin's fists clenched at his side. Even more reason to get his own justice.

Torin straightened. "Thank you for telling me, Mr. Sampson. It means a lot, but I really need to get moving."

"Just think about what you're about to do, young Torin. Be sure of it."

Torin nodded. "I am sure. But thank you. Can I see Kira now?"

"I don't think you should. She's resting and will still be here when you get back. Don't worry, we'll take good care of her." He gave Torin's shoulder a squeeze.

"I'd still like to see her though; will she be okay?" The butler had already proven himself more supportive than Torin's own father ever was. He wanted to tell the old man everything, but couldn't risk it.

"Mrs. Young says she has a good chance. But she's not out of the woods. She's in the maid's room by Mrs. Young's quarters, resting. No need to worry. We won't tell your father about this, not yet anyway. You just deal with one problem at a time." His father would probably be pleased to hear what he'd done.

"Okay, I'll go."

The truth was, he was scared to see Kira. Scared he would never see the light in her eyes again.

He felt physically sick at the thought of leaving her like this, but he was no help here, anyway. At least if he left, he could do something right, he could avenge his mother's death and bring a little peace to his family. He could make all their lives better in the future, including Kira's. His only choice was to get on with the mission.

When he got back, she would be alive and probably hating him, which was fine. She just had to be alive. Though now he was starting to doubt whether he should leave tonight or wait till he knew she would be okay.

"Just keep your wits about you. Don't worry about young Kira."

Torin nodded and inhaled deeply as he stood. Mr. Sampson hustled him out the door with a heartfelt "Happy Birthday." Torin hesitated for a second outside the maid's door but kept walking. He was a coward. But he was going to make things right.

Chapter 10

Torin ran back to his room to grab his dinner jacket. He flung it over his shoulder and tucked his elemer into his belt, then marched upstairs to the front door as he caught his breath before stepping into the cool evening air. The sky was already darkening, and everything smelled of fresh rain on earth. He was low on energy, and all he could think about was Kira.

How the hell was he going to get through this mission? How did he let himself do that? He didn't deserve this power, this *gift,* as his father called it. It was nothing but a curse, but a curse he needed to use one more time to set things right. Then he was done. He'd wear gloves for the rest of his life, never touch another human again, even stop using Shadow Magic if that's what it took to control this gods-forsaken power.

He stood up straight and marched across to his father who was waiting by the gate to the garden.

"About bloody time." His father's voice rang out in the still evening air.

Strange. The storm from before was long gone, and the air was fragrant with jasmine. Even the birds were quiet. Either everything was calm, maybe a good sign from his mother, or everything was about to go horribly wrong.

"Sorry. I'm ready now." He clasped his elemer and dropped his hands to—hopefully—appear natural at his sides. His face was set to the stony mask he needed it to be.

"You appear anything *but* ready. Do you understand this is the biggest moment of your life?"

His father saw through him. Of course he wasn't ready. Kira was lying there dying, and here he was, skipping off to take a life. If this was the way things were going, he wouldn't be surprised if the prophecies were true and he started a series of world disasters.

"Of course, Father. It's about time those snake bastards got a taste of their own medicine," he said, knowing that's all his father wanted to hear.

"Good lad. You've come a long way, but it's yet to be seen if you've got what it takes. Now let's get a move on." His father's overly polished boots crunched into the gravel as he cut into the Hollow.

A flash of black caught Torin's eye. He glanced toward the house. A raven sat on the highest turret spire, glaring down at him against the sky of darkening purple.

His father nodded, seeing where Torin's gaze fell. "A good omen." He nodded approvingly as he held the door to the darkness.

A good omen. Torin knew what it really meant—death.

Perhaps tonight would close the loop and balance things. He squared his shoulders and followed his father.

It was a strange, eerie feeling, just the two of them in the sub-dimensional void. He almost wished a shadow wraith or demon would show up just to break the silence. But his father didn't seem to notice and wasted no time in cutting to a new location somewhere else in England, though Torin had no idea where. Apparently, the House of Snakes manor's location was need-to-know information, and Torin's pay grade wasn't high enough.

They stepped out to the same dark purple sky with heavy clouds, and his father wasted no time in marching toward a shiny black Land Rover that awaited on the side of the road. One of many identical ones in his new fleet. The man had a lot of cars.

Torin was right behind him. Sliding into the back seat next to his father, he forced his mask of confidence back up when he noticed his father watching him.

"I won't let you down, Father."

"You better not," his father warned and looked out the window.

Car tires bit into gravel, and Torin's back pressed into the firm leather seats that smelled far too new. There was no going back now.

It took over an hour to reach the edge of the House of Snakes' estate from wherever they were. An hour that felt more like three. They spent half the journey going over every element of the plan. His father drilled him over tiny details: where Torin would place the bugs, how he would navigate the house, where to look for *The Shadow Atlas*, how he would approach the Viper, how he would take him down, how he would get out again. They'd been over it as many times as they could.

The other half of the journey was silence. Trapped in the backseat of the expensive four-by-four was like being in a luxury coffin. Deathly quiet and suffocating.

Being alone with his thoughts was the last thing Torin needed. He pushed his finger into his palm, hoping this was all a dream. It wasn't. He couldn't get the image of Kira's blank eyes staring up at him out of his mind, the way they'd drilled through him as if he wasn't even there.

The vehicle stopped, and like a programmed robot, Torin got out of the car. They were at the meeting point.

The evening sky had turned from purple to deep inky gray and blue. The air was rich with fragrant honeysuckle from the numerous hedgerows. Again, he caught a whiff of jasmine, and for a second his thoughts turned to a memory of his mother. He saw her flicking her long black hair over her shoulder as she reached down to smell the blossoms that crept over the wall. He let his shoulders relax.

Tonight, she would finally be free.

His father's glare burned through him as if to say, *get a fucking move on*. He moved, not because of that, but because they needed to stay hidden.

A corrugated iron shed leaned against a half-toppled stone wall. He avoided the jagged bits of rust as he followed his father behind the structure that looked like a weak breeze would knock it down.

The Land Rover sped off. This was weird. Crouching behind a crappy shed with his father was very un-Korbyn Dumont. He never got his hands dirty. There were other people for that.

Torin supposed he should feel honored his father was bringing himself this low to supervise his test.

You can do this Torin. Do it for Mum . . . and maybe for his father as well. He let out a shaky breath as a convoy of cars rumbled past. *Pep talk over.* He needed to concentrate.

A constant stream of traffic flowed up the narrow country lane, all going to the House of Snakes headquarters for the party tonight, not a council meeting as he had originally been told. Guests, catering, flowers, ice sculptures of giant serpents—or whatever it was arsehole Snakes ordered for their parties—all rolled by. It turned out this frivolity was part of his father's plan to get Torin inside.

Serpent mages would be monitoring the area for any unexplained use of magic for security reasons, hence their slow trip there. So, their best bet was to get in the old-fashioned way: hiding in a van.

Five tense minutes later, the van turned up. Checking that the coast was clear, Torin nodded to his father as the side door slid open. They both darted from their hiding spot and slipped in, folding themselves away in the back corner. The aroma of fresh bread made Torin's mouth water. He hadn't eaten since early that morning, but a churning stomach of nerves told him it would be a bad idea. Eating at his ceremony at the Rook would be his reward once all this was over, then he would finally leave.

"The bugs. There are ten. Plant as many as you can before anyone enters the room." His father handed him a leather pouch, heavier than expected.

"Ten? We agreed to four. Why the change in plans?" Now was not the time to be adding new information and new tasks. Four was a safe number to plant in the time he'd have in the room before anyone should enter. Ten was risky.

"Don't question my reasons, boy. Just do as you're told."

Torin plucked out a bug and rolled it in his palm. It was far larger than their standard devices. Still, it should be easy enough to conceal, and he assumed they had the same cloaking charms as the usual ones. They'd only be noticed if someone was looking very hard.

"Getting cold feet, are you?"

"Course not."

"Good. And don't forget to look for *The Shadow Atlas*. I want it back."

Another ten minutes of bumping down pothole-filled roads, and the van stopped.

"This is my stop," his father said. "Make me proud, boy."

Torin gave a firm nod. His father slapped his shoulder and slid out of the van like a shadow wraith.

This was it. Torin was alone in the van, heading for enemy territory. *Was he doing the right thing?* A little late to reconsider now.

The van bumped along for another minute. Torin squished himself into the corner and snatched a gingham tablecloth from a shelf to drape over himself as the brakes creaked and ground to a halt. He held his breath as the van door slid open.

"It's the rules, mate. Got to check every van and lorry coming in," a voice shouted.

Torchlight bounced around the shelves lined with rows of bread and pastries. Torin didn't dare use a shadow cloak in case they were detecting for magic. Hopefully, his gingham disguise was better than nothing.

"Got a cheeky pastry in there, mate? I'm starving," a gruff voice from outside said.

Another set of footsteps moved closer.

"Why not? One Danish won't hurt 'em." The driver chuckled. Nothing like free food to get on someone's good side.

A second later, pastry crunched, and the door slammed shut.

The van spluttered back into life, and they were inside the grounds of the House of Snakes.

Chapter 11

After a short drive, the van shuddered to a stop, and Torin pressed himself into the corner awaiting instruction. Presumably, they had stopped outside the servants' entrance. That would explain the prattle of voices and the sound of carts clattering around on bumpy stone. After a few heavy footsteps, the door swung open, and the aroma of flowers mingled with the smells of garlic and other mouthwatering dinner fragrances rushed in.

"Here, put this on, then help me unload the truck." The driver threw something toward Torin's corner. Well hidden behind a rack of shelves, he didn't waste any time putting on the formal waiter's uniform, complete with bowtie and white gloves. He draped his own jacket neatly in the corner and secured the bugs in his new jacket pocket.

Standing, he brushed himself off and grabbed a tray of amazing-looking custard tarts on his way out, regretting not having eaten any on the ride over.

He helped the driver unload the pastries into the large service kitchen, noting every person he passed as he did so. Fortunately, it was busy enough he could slip in as another server.

The driver shut the van door after their final tray was unloaded and spoke in a low voice.

"You've got one hour. I left a tray in the kitchen storeroom with tins I need to bring back. When you're done, grab the tray and put it in the back of the van, and I'll shut you back in. No one will notice."

Torin nodded, and without another word, he marched through the back door, down a hallway, and around the corner into the chaotic kitchen as if he was meant to be there. Pots bubbled, food sizzled, and people were yelling in all directions. He tried to remain inconspicuous as he assessed the room and planned where he needed to get to.

There were serving trays already laid out with food, a perfect opportunity to get close to the crowd, maybe plant some of the additional bugs in the main room. Extra surveillance couldn't hurt. Plus, he wanted to see these people, their supposed enemies.

"You lad, take this one out now." A bloke in a suit the same as his handed him a tray of effervescent champagne flutes.

"Where to?" Torin asked as he took the weight of the tray. Okay, so maybe being a server wasn't as easy as he first assumed. *How the hell do they carry these with one hand?*

"The ballroom. Offer them to the guests, then come straight back," the man said in a sharp tone, looking down at Torin's two-handed grasp on the tray. "And for gods' sake, hold it properly."

The man spun around to yell at the next lackey to come along.

Torin made his way through a second kitchen, this one less industrial but filled with mouth-watering desserts that made him want to stop, especially for a lemon tart. *Don't get distracted by food.* He could never say no to lemon tarts, but this time he stayed strong. With a watering mouth, he looked away and followed the sound of laughter and music down a long hallway, straight toward what should be the drawing room.

It surprised him how calm he was, how clear and focused everything had become. Each footstep secured in his mind that he was doing the right thing. He made his way through the drawing room where small groups were chatting away, taking no notice of him. At the other end of the room was the library where the council would meet later. He took note of the door and how far he would have to walk to gain access.

Balancing the tray on one hand, he veered the opposite way and neared the loud ballroom, copying the gait and stance of the server in front of him. He patted the inside of his jacket pocket to feel the bugs were there.

Orchestral music flowed into him as he turned into the ballroom, making him want to be part of it. The music, not the ball. He hated gatherings like this but missed playing the piano. Apparently, it wasn't a useful enough skill in his father's eyes.

The room wasn't as large or as grand as the ballroom at the Rook, but it was vibrant and full of life. Graceful dancers waltzed around the parquet floor, all smiles and laughter, and above them, oversized chandeliers sparkled and lit the room with a warm glow. Around the edge of the room, people mingled in the spaces between large tropical palms in giant gold pots, and along them were endless rows of tables of tiny foods and bubbly drinks.

No wonder the kitchen was so busy keeping up with this lot.

Torin breezed through a crowd of glamorous ladies like a ghost, their only interest in his stems of champagne. He waded amidst a cloud of perfume as he did his best not to stare at the tattoos on their bare arms. It surprised him at how openly they displayed them, especially when they were such varying levels of power. A few had tattoos so small they could barely be mages. *Weren't they embarrassed?*

It was a rare sight for mages to have their tattoos exposed so openly, but he supposed they felt like they were in safe company. In the House of Ravens, it was considered a weakness to show anyone your tattoos. It was giving people a look inside yourself, showing them your vulnerabilities or strengths, a stupid thing to give away up front.

It was also surprising that many of the women in these beautiful dresses weren't mages at all. There were non-magic people here. How very odd. There were also mages from other houses. He spotted tattoos from the House of Eagles, House of Bees, House of the White Deer, and House of the Winged Bull but didn't notice any Phoenixes or Owls about. Of course, there was no one from the House of Ravens. Though he couldn't be sure, as the men wore tuxedos, so it wasn't exactly a fair survey.

He forced himself to stop staring and went back to scanning the room.

As he eyed up places to plant a bug, he couldn't stop thinking how odd it was to have all these houses mingling together. This certainly wasn't a House of Snakes party and council session like his father had told him.

But no matter, he had a job to do and couldn't get caught up worrying about House politics now. He needed to get near the tables on the edge, which appeared to be a congregation spot.

There were only four glasses left on his tray. He nearly had a heart attack when someone swiped one from the edge and his tray wobbled, verging on being flipped. He snapped his hand up and steadied it just in time.

Amateur move. He needed to be a lot more vigilant. How was holding a tray so much harder than it looked? The servants at the Rook needed more credit. It was no wonder his father went through staff so fast.

The table was close now, but he needed to be clever about this. He kept his face neutral and offered his last drinks to a group standing right by the towers of tiny cakes with flowers on top. They took the glasses but returned their empty ones to his tray. *Bugger*. Now what?

He spotted another server coming his way with full glasses. He couldn't use any magic; it was too risky in a room full of mages.

Tripping, it was. Torin moved closer to the plant he eyed up for his bug and bumped into a man behind him; the man swung around and conveniently knocked the server's tray from his hand, sending the glasses crashing to the floor.

"So sorry, dear boy." The old man turned around, looking genuinely startled. Torin crouched next to the plant and slipped the bug out of his jacket pocket. As he leaned over, he pressed it into the rim of the pot before turning back to clean up the mess.

"Not to worry," an oldish man with a showy mustache said loudly. He aimed his elemer at the glass in a flamboyant fashion and swirled it up into a vortex of glittering glass.

"Thank you, sir, so sorry about that," Torin said as two more servers came to help. No one was looking at him now. Clearly, the man cleaning up the glass was a showman. His dazzling grin and speckled gray hair had everyone enthralled as he twisted the broken glass up into the air in a spectacle of light reflecting off the chandeliers. *Thanks for the distraction, mate.*

Couldn't have been better timing. Torin slipped back out with his empty tray.

With the blueprints of the manor house seared into his mind from years of studying them obsessively, Torin stepped out of the ballroom and straight through the less populated drawing room with the confidence of someone who knew where they were going. He checked his watch. Still making good time, but he had to be quick about this.

He slid out his elemer and opened the door at the end without knocking. If anyone asked, he would say he was lost. Fortunately, no one was in there. It was still thirty minutes until the scheduled meeting, and he would be long gone by then.

Torin slipped in quietly. The room was like any other dated country house study: stuffy, with lots of red decor, a few animal heads, and dark wood. Red and gold curtains framed the tall windows, and leather books lined the ceiling-high shelves.

He made his way around the room, wasting no time in setting the bugs in the numerous twenties-style lamps as well as in the bookshelves, under a rug, in several more plants, and under the large oak table at the center of the room. They didn't need to be subtle. They should be well-cloaked for a few weeks at least. After that, it didn't matter if they were discovered; they would have served their purpose.

Torin suspected his father wanted to overhear the plans from the new leadership once Torin took out the Viper. Maybe in the chaos and panic, they would reveal some vital information his father had been searching for or perhaps lead to a clue about *The Shadow Atlas*.

He could imagine his father at the edge of the property right now, waiting to listen in live as soon as Torin got back to him.

As he made his way around, he scoured the shelves and desk for *The Shadow Atlas*, but as suspected, it was nowhere in sight. If the book was that important, he hardly expected to find it lying around.

He checked his watch. He had five minutes to spare before the Viper himself would enter the room to prepare for the meeting. That was what their intel told them, anyway. Torin crouched behind a green velvet armchair and waited. It was a perfect spot. Anyone entering wouldn't see him, and it was far enough from the door that they would have to close it and walk a few meters before Torin could spring on them.

Torin didn't have time to prepare any further before the door swung open. One man entered alone. *The Viper.* The man he had waited so many years to see in this very moment.

Torin watched as if this was a movie in slow motion, surreal. The Viper had dark hair that hung past his shoulders, and he wore a very expensive tuxedo. He was much taller than Torin expected, but his face held a hint of a smile like he'd just found out some really good news and couldn't contain it.

Rage welled up in Torin's chest. This man didn't deserve to be happy. He didn't deserve this giant house filled with smiling faces and fine food. Not when Torin didn't have a mother because of him. Nothing could make up for that.

Before he knew it, Torin was on the move. All his careful planning was out the window as his elemer warmed in his hand like it knew what he was thinking. He cut into the Shadow Dimension and ripped the magic through his body, throwing it straight at the man before he had time to react. The Viper's whiskey glass slipped from his fingers and smashed to the ground as Torin fueled his magic with anger.

He hit the man with a string of shadow ropes and kicked his elemer from his hand. It was clear he had been drinking, too comfortable and complacent in his own home.

But Torin's mind was clearer than it had ever been. His magic was sharp and not dulled by alcohol, unlike this supposedly powerful shadow mage.

"You're pathetic," Torin yelled as his ropes bound the man. The smile had vanished from his face now.

"You don't need to do this, son." The man spoke calmly, his voice all silk and lies. It only drove the rage deeper into Torin's blood, strengthening his magic.

"I am not your son." He ground his teeth.

"I know who you are, and I knew this day would come. I knew your father would poison your mind enough to send you to do his dirty work." This idiot was lying on the ground, bound in shadows. How could he be this arrogant? He was asking for this.

"If you know who I am, then you know why I'm here," Torin said

"I do. Let me go, and I can help you."

So that was his plan now. Try to recruit him to his side. *Pathetic.*

"You don't get a say in this." Torin wanted to lunge forward and punch the Viper in his stupid bearded face but resisted. He had to get this over with. He shouldn't even let the guy talk.

"You murdered my mother. I'm here to set the balance," Torin said as calmly as he could. He took off one of the white gloves, trying to suppress the shake in his hand as he pressed it hard into the man's chest. The beat of his heart pulsed right through Torin, remaining slow and steady, even facing death.

Why wasn't this man fighting him? He had expected more of the great Viper.

What he wanted to do was strangle the man and make him feel every second of his death, but there wasn't time. He needed to get this over with and done right, without emotion ruining his judgment.

"This is for my mother."

The man jerked up, fighting the shadow bonds with a strength Torin had never felt. It was as if his magic was drawing from the shadows Torin made.

Blasts of darkness shot from the man's hands and threw Torin across the room. All without an elemer. Torin didn't have time to think. He rolled behind a red sofa and stood. His shadow ropes still pinned the man to the ground, so he threw more energy into his magic and extended the ropes to cover the man's hands with inky darkness.

He marched across the room and leaned over him, pushing hard into the man's chest. "That's enough," Torin yelled.

"Please don't hurt anyone else." A faint whisper came from his lips, and his gray eyes locked on to Torin, unblinking. It was unnerving, but Torin didn't look away.

He did his best to block out the man's voice. His heartbeat slowed with each breath. Sweat dripped down his forehead and onto the man's tux. At this moment, he was grateful for his new gift. The previous plan involved knives—a lot messier. This was humane at least, and something he would never have to do again after tonight.

Torin didn't respond. He had no intention of hurting anyone else. Yes, the House of Snakes was their enemy, but his grudge was only with this man. Perhaps with a new leader, they could all find peace and end this ridiculous feuding.

"This wasn't how it was supposed to go," the man wheezed. "You will bring darkness on us all."

"You're wrong. This will bring balance to us all," Torin whispered.

The man's stare crept into his soul in those few seconds as his life slipped away. His eyes filled with sorrow, regret, and pride, but there was no hatred or fear.

"Your mother wouldn't have wanted this. She . . . It was your father . . ."

His last heartbeat ticked over.

His father what? Torin's heart clenched in his chest as bile rose in his throat. He almost didn't want to know. How would this man know what Torin's mother would have wanted? What had his father done?

A spike of unease shot up his spine. Had he made a mistake? Could his father have been the one to—? No. He refused to think about it.

This was not the triumphant moment of euphoria he had expected.

But it was done, and finally, Yelena Dumont could rest in peace. He wished there was a grave he could visit to tell her.

He went to stand up but stumbled back and fell against a side table, knocking over a lamp, realizing the exertion the spell had taken. His shirt was soaked through with sweat, and his hands were shaking uncontrollably. That had been much harder than the rabbits or Licorice . . . or Kira.

The shadow ropes he had been maintaining around the man faded away to nothing, and his limp arms fell to the ground. His jacket hung open.

Torin sat up. His brain was dulled, but he forced himself to think about what to do next. The book? Perhaps he kept *The Shadow Atlas* close to him? One last check, then he could escape. He searched through the Viper's jacket with trembling hands. The only thing he found was a silver pocket watch. Flicking open the latch revealed a photo of a serious-looking girl with brown hair, around ten years old, he guessed. The Viper's daughter?

Good. This girl would know what it was like to lose a parent, just as he had. *Balance.*

He snapped the watch shut and tucked it into the man's pocket.

No book, but definitely time to get out of here.

Chapter 12

The van cleared the gates with no issues. And just like that Torin was out, his heart drumming like a storm in his chest as he slipped out of the waiters' uniform and back into his new dinner suit. He busied himself attaching his House of Ravens cufflinks onto his pristine white sleeves, and it was only a minute until the van slowed to where they'd dropped off his father.

A banging sounded on the van's side. "Your stop, mate."

Torin slipped from his corner, the door opened, and he jumped out. He thanked the driver as if it were a simple taxi ride and adjusted his suit as he headed toward the trees.

"Did you succeed?" His father's voice came from the darkened tree line.

There was no, *are you okay, son? Are you mentally scarred, son?* But *did you succeed?* As cold and blunt as the fake sword that hung in his office.

Torin walked into the shadows. "I did it." His mouth was dry. This was all wrong. Shouldn't he be happy right now? Shouldn't he feel on top of the world or like he was the master of death or something? Maybe it was because he couldn't stop thinking about Kira.

"Good." All his father offered was a stiff nod of his head. "Follow me."

Torin glanced around and kept his elemer ready at his side before following his father into the trees. Gods knew where. He probably wanted to be close to listen in on the aftermath of discovering the body. Torin was not so keen.

They trudged through overgrown damp grass before they came to a tall fence topped with razor wire. There was a clear view of the large white country house, but Torin and his father remained hidden in the shadows of the trees, no need for magic. They took a seat on a sturdy log.

"Why are we here?" Torin asked.

"You'll see. Be patient." His father checked his watch and pulled out his laptop, setting it up on his knees with a grin that made the hairs on the back of Torin's neck lift.

"Now, tell me how it went. Here, have some of this." His father pulled a flask from his jacket pocket.

"What is it?" Torin wasn't sure if he should trust anything his father gave him to drink.

"It's whiskey."

Nodding in thanks, Torin took a sip hoping to numb out what he had done. His throat burned, and a cough bubbled up from his lungs. *Nasty.* He handed the flask back. His father frowned at his lack of drinking skills but said nothing.

It was a miracle he'd even been allowed a drink.

The alcohol burned in his empty stomach but gave him the extra bit of courage he needed to recount the events to his father and remain detached. It was as if he were telling someone else's story—the only way he could get through this. He relayed every detail until when he stopped the Viper's heart.

It felt like it hadn't been him doing it. Like it was all a weird dream, and it was good to do something right for a change, though it was hard to shake the sense of unease that perhaps something wasn't right . . .

His father looked down at his watch and back to his computer. Torin wasn't familiar with the surveillance program his father had opened.

"Why doesn't Mum have a grave?" Torin asked as the question popped into his head out of the blue.

His father frowned but didn't look up. "The answer is the same as the other hundred times you asked. She was cremated."

"But why isn't there a memorial or something for her?"

"There just isn't," Korbyn snapped.

But why? He knew better than to ask again.

"At least she can rest in peace now," Torin said, his eyes trained on his father.

"I suppose," Korbyn said, concentrating on the screen.

Torin's lip curled back in disgust. *That's all he had to say?* He wanted to shake his father, wanted him to show some sort of emotion that wasn't related to hatred or power. Was he that far gone?

A change in tactics was warranted, one last chance for his father to prove he wasn't the monster Torin was beginning to see him as.

"Why did you kill that shaman?" If he had a legitimate answer, there was still hope.

"He had something I wanted," Korbyn said, still not looking up.

"You couldn't have just asked for it?"

"No, dear boy," he said mockingly. "Well, actually, I asked for it, but the old coot refused to give it up." He shook his head and sneered.

This man had no remorse, no empathy, no heart. Torin couldn't look at him. His flesh crawled as he imagined all the things his father might have done to the poor man to get whatever it was.

"What was it? The item?"

"This fine elemer." He held up his elemer proudly.

Torin had seen it before but never asked about it. It was white bone with several gemstones in the handle. It didn't look overly valuable or rare. He was sure he didn't want to know anything more, but his father continued.

"It contains alexandrite, a rare stone in an elemer, but its dual properties allow it to easily control both Echo and Shadow Magic. Its handle is made from the bones of a great shadow mage. It belongs with our House, and one day it will be yours."

What the fuck? No thanks. Nothing as stupid as this could be worth killing that sweet old shaman. How could he have been blind to it this whole time?

"It's in worthy hands now," Torin forced himself to say. He could do this, play along until he got back and could make a plan to leave.

"Ready, my boy. Any second now."

This was it. They were about to discover the body, and then they could go.

They sat in silence. The sounds of the night went on around them: crickets chirping, the faint rustle of trees, distant laughter from the party . . .

But it all shattered in an instant—BOOM!

Torin fell back, his hand scraping the bark of a tree behind him from the deafening blast. The explosion sent a pulse through the night, fracturing the calm and pitching everything into darkness. Then the screams started.

"What the fuck was that?" Torin said over his ringing ears. Switching to alert mode, he was on his feet in seconds, ready to react despite having no idea what was going on.

Wails of pain and grief echoed across the parkland between them and the house.

His father chuckled.

"What did you do?" Torin asked, his eyes wide as he stared at his father.

"You mean what did *you* do?" He stared at the house with a grin that made Torin want to vomit. Plumes of smoke rose in columns from the windows of the large country house.

What had he done?

"The bugs I had you place in the study were explosive devices. They appear to have all activated successfully." He slammed his computer shut and tucked it back into his bag. "Good show. Hopefully, they took out the House of Snakes council and some of those stuffy allies of theirs in the process," he said with a smirk.

Explosive devices! What the fuck? A sickening horror washed over Torin. *How had he not known that? Why didn't he look at the bugs closely? Wasn't one death enough?* One deserved death was what he'd signed up for. And now he was questioning even that. Killing innocent people was not on his agenda.

"This . . . but why . . . what about all the other people?" His voice rose in panic. Torin tried to block out the screams from across the field. He fought his instincts to jump the fence and try to help people get out. That would seal his own death warrant.

"I'm not a monster. It was only a few council members. The world will be a better place without them."

"I put bugs in the ballroom as well," Torin said. He balked, imagining all those happy people now with shredded skin and torn limbs strewn across the ballroom.

His father smirked; his eyes lit up with sick delight. "Well done, my boy."

This was beyond wrong. Torin had ignored so many things in the past, rationalized them by believing it was for the greater good, for the benefit of the House of Ravens. Believing he could help his father find peace. But he was sixteen, today in fact, and his eyes were wide open.

"You used me." He threw his hands up to his head and closed his eyes in realization.

"Now, now. No need for dramatics. The job is done, and I will make you an apprentice tonight. We must celebrate." Korbyn reached for Torin's shoulder.

Torin recoiled from the outstretched hand.

In that second, he knew he had to leave and had to own up to everything. There was no running away. No new identity and no secret life as a normal person. He would not cover up for his father, and he sure as hell wouldn't become this monster. If he had to sacrifice himself and his future to reset the balance, then so be it, but he was taking his father down with him.

First, he had to get himself under control. He still had to play along and get through the rest of the night—he still had to say goodbye to Kira.

Taking a calming breath, he nodded. "You're right, Father. It's hard to believe it all went as planned. Better even," he lied, forcing himself to relax, to appear fully in control and not a mess of self-doubt and guilt.

"And to think I ever doubted you," his father said.

Screams echoed in the air, and the sound of sirens grew closer in the distance. The smell of smoke singed Torin's nostrils, making him want to gag.

"Better get on with it. Cut into the Hollow, and let's get to your party."

His party? That was the last thing he needed.

Chapter 13

Torin hardly noticed the trip back. Having no need to hide their magical signatures anymore, he used the dregs of his magic to open into the Hollow, and he mindlessly followed his father back to the Rook.

Cheers rang out as they stepped from the darkness into the jasmine garden and the waiting crowd. Several guards did a poor job of hiding the relief in their eyes when they saw Torin. Mage Emerson hugged him, which only meant one thing—if he had failed, he wouldn't have been returning at all.

There must have been a signal when he arrived, because fireworks exploded from the ramparts of the castle. The ravens burst from the north tower and escaped into the night as colored light exploded into the sky.

Everything about this is wrong. He didn't deserve a celebration. For all he knew, he'd just murdered a ballroom full of innocent people, and he suspected others here knew it too. Suddenly his suit was too tight, and the air was too hot.

Marching on autopilot, a parade of bizarre jubilation led him into the Rook. His father's arm hung around his shoulders, steering him the right way, which made this whole thing stranger.

"You didn't think I'd forget your birthday, did you, boy?"

No, you were waiting to see if it was worth celebrating or if you were going to exile me or kill me, you bastard.

"Course not. I had bigger things on my mind, anyway," Torin replied, barely keeping it together. He wanted nothing more than to rip his father's arm off and accuse him of mass murder.

"Too right, son."

Son. The word he had wanted to hear his whole life came out bitter and poisoned in the light of new truths.

They herded him into the grand hall like a prized pig at the fair. Tables were covered with white candles, flower arrangements of lilies and baby's breath, and ivory tablecloths that made the whole thing look like a bloody wedding. Aromas of roast beef and garlic hit him before he spotted the mountains of food. Crisp potatoes, vibrant vegetables, and even a pig on the spit. All spread out in a feast like something out of a movie.

But eating was the last thing on Torin's mind. His mouth was dry, and the whiskey was sloshing around in his stomach.

Getting this ceremony over with was the only thing he needed to focus on. After that, the rest would have to unfurl with the guidance of the universe—in other words—winging it. All he knew was that he had to see Kira. He had to know she would be okay.

Matt, Dev, and Conner were near the bar set up on the other side of the hall, standing around looking bored. A good sign, because if Kira was dead, they either wouldn't be there or would be heading straight for him with pitchforks.

People went by in a blur, shaking his hands, slapping him on the back, congratulating him, and asking him to regale them with his story, but his father waved them all off, directing Torin straight to the front of the long room.

They stopped on the raised dais at the front. His father cleared his throat, and the hundred or so people instantly fell silent.

Torin looked around, standing tall like the son of the great Korbyn Dumont was expected to, knowing these people were only here either to impress his father or out of fear of being on the wrong side if there was ever a House war.

Scanning the crowd, he noted most of the people were from the House of Ravens—mages, distant relatives, and overseas counterparts that were still loyal to his father. They didn't show their tattoos, but all had some form of insignia with a raven on them: broaches, necklaces, and embroidered family crests. Several of the older men had canes similar to his father's.

Torin put on his *I'm ready to be an apprentice* face. Serious and confident, staring down anyone who dared look him in the eye. He had learned a thing or two all these years watching his father.

The ceremony began, and Torin's eyes glazed over as his father spoke of the long and glorious history of the House of Ravens. Meanwhile, Torin agonized over what words to say to Kira. Nothing came close to good enough. How could he even begin to apologize for what he had done?

He realized the hall was silent.

"Torin?" His father cleared his throat.

Crap, he was supposed to be doing something.

His father tapped his cane loudly on the floor and nodded to the man behind him. A servant dressed in old-timey livery—no doubt for the theatrics of it—stepped toward Torin carrying a blue velvet cushion with a tiny vial on top.

Torin's stomach dropped. He hadn't thought about this part. He had been so busy over the past few days, he might have blocked it out on purpose. Either way, he hadn't had time to think about how horrible this might be. Probably better that way.

He swallowed hard as the man near him bowed his head, offering the cushion's charge to Torin.

Torin slid his elemer into his belt and picked up the vial with steady hands.

"I am overjoyed to present Recruit Torin Dumont with the elixir of the gods. May it give him strength and courage in his new position as apprentice. Zakar, give him strength," His father's voice boomed across the room.

"Zakar, give him strength," the voices of the Raven flock echoed back.

Torin took a shaky breath. This was it. The glass was cold in his palm. The tiny lid was a carved raven, and within, the inky blue liquid had a luminescent sheen as it swirled around the edges.

"I accept the elixir of the gods and pledge myself as apprentice to the House of Ravens," he said, surprised at how steady his voice rang out while his insides turned to jelly. The pledge wasn't a lie. He meant every word; he wasn't turning on the House of Ravens. He was going to make them better. It might take a while, but he would be back.

Applause erupted through the crowd, and whistles shrilled loudly—probably his squad mates—as Torin extracted the glass stopper and downed the liquid in one go.

The effect was instant. His head rolled back, and he collapsed. His last memory was of the spinning beams of the ceiling.

A familiar blocky pyramid rose out of the sand in front of him, and the hot desert air sent ripples of heat over his exposed skin. He closed his eyes and relished the warmth of the two suns beating down on him, loosening his muscles, drawing him into a false sense of security. He noticed his chest was bare, and there was a rectangular cloth draped around his hips, just enough to cover all his bits.

It was just a dream, and he was perfectly comfortable.

Forcing his eyes to stay focused, he looked around, but everything blurred in a lazy haze. He had been here before, the Great Desert of Dreams ruled by the god Zakar. This was part of the test, and he had to stay alert and endure whatever was coming.

Kira appeared in front of him on the long marble path that led into the desert. Thin lavender robes billowed around her in the scorching wind.

"Kira." He reached out but found himself unable to move.

Fiery eyes that weren't her own drilled into him.

"You were never good enough for me, Torin. I want to be with Conner."

His throat was dry. Sand whipped up, blasting him from every angle as he ordered his feet to move. He looked down to see they had become part of the marble.

No noise came out as he screamed. Kira turned and dissolved into sand that swept straight into the sky.

A woman appeared in her place. His mother. Her long black hair tangled around her in the wind like seaweed hiding her face.

"Why do you never visit my grave, my dear child?" Her voice was exactly how he remembered it but filled with unmistakable sorrow.

"I'm sorry, Mum. There is no grave."

"Find me . . ." She collapsed into a pile of sand and trickled across the marble, back into the desert as if she had never been.

This isn't real. He had to stay calm so he could get back. He couldn't lose it now or he'd become trapped in this world.

The Viper appeared next, standing with his arms crossed. He wore the same strip of cloth, so all his tattoos were on display. They covered every inch of his body, a combination of snakes, vines, dragons, and flowers all woven into a glorious artwork that demonstrated his true power. How had Torin been able to take down a man with this mastery? Just a dream, he reminded himself.

"I was not the one to kill your mother. You know in your heart who the true murderer is. You will pay for what you have done." His eyes turned dark, and he sprinted at Torin, his elemer raised above his head for the kill.

Torin was too slow. He raised his arm, but the attack never came. He was blasted with sand that picked up speed, driving into his skin as it turned into a tornado around him.

A man stepped out. Not a man. A god.

Twice the height of Torin, the god Zakar stood before him. The wind died down to nothing.

Torin tasted sand, and the grit in his mouth stole away his saliva. The smell of the baking stone rippled in the heat as he knelt before his god.

Zakar looked like a champion weightlifter. His muscles rippled with golden skin that reflected the sun, and his face was hard-lined and battle-worn. Despite being thousands of years old, he only had a hint of salt and pepper coloring through his beard to show for it while his long hair remained black.

"You are worthy, Torin Dumont, son of the House of Ravens. I see your heart and know it is true."

"Thank you, Lord Zakar."

"Drink from the cup, and accept what is to come."

Torin's mind was floaty. All he could do was accept and hope he made it back. A wooden cup appeared before him. He was so thirsty he grabbed it and drank deeply, knowing the next part would hurt.

Searing pain struck his legs, and his guts clenched as his shoulder hit the solid marble.

"Go well, son of the Ravens," Zakar said as Torin's vision flashed black and red.

The pain was like nothing he had ever felt. Every nerve in his body fired as his back arched, and he let out a scream.

The heat was suddenly gone. Cold air rushed over him, and someone was shaking his shoulder.

He opened his eyes to see his father looming over him.

"He has awakened and passed the test!" His father shouted, and a roar erupted around him.

That was right, he was at the ceremony, still. It was just a dream. How long was he out for? He needed to get to Kira.

Panic seized his body along with a fresh wave of pain. Ouch. So, some of the dream was real. His whole body ached like he'd been tossed around in a tornado and flung out the other side.

He sat up, and the servant in his ridiculous costume handed Torin some water. He had never been so grateful in his life.

The crowd drifted toward the food as Torin gained his bearings. His father was deep in conversation with some important-looking people; this was Torin's chance to escape. He had passed everything. He was now worthy of his House, but it was time to go.

He nodded to his father as he took baby steps to get off the small stage. Eyes focused on the doorway that led down to the kitchens, he shuffled his way over as the feeling came back to his legs. He smiled and accepted handshakes from the random strangers who seemed to know who he was.

Just a few more meters to the door.

"Where do you think you're sneaking off to?" Conner stepped into Torin's path.

Dev and Matt swooped in from either side.

"Congratulations, mate," Dev said, shaking Torin's hand.

"Yeah, good one. At least one of us has made it now," Matt added enthusiastically and gave Torin a big hug. He stepped back and gave Conner a not-so-subtle sideways glance.

"Do you have something to say, Conner?" Torin asked, overly polite.

"Congratulations, man," he said and, to Torin's surprise, reached out and shook his hand. Instantly aware of the steady heartbeat in Conner's palm, he broke away quickly.

"Thanks, lads, but I don't have time to chat right now." Torin inched toward the door.

"Hold up, mate. Aren't you going to regale us with tales of your victory?" Conner asked, somewhat sarcastically.

"Certainly. But right now, I have somewhere to be."

"It's your birthday and apprentice ceremony, Torin. You literally have nowhere else to be," Conner said, crossing his arms.

"It wouldn't have something to do with Kira, would it? We can't find her anywhere, and it's not like her to miss a party for you," Dev said.

Torin forced his shoulders back as his body threatened to collapse into a pathetic pool of liquid around him. He wished more than anything that she was here.

His squad mates' glares lasered in on him, waiting for an answer. He took in a shaky breath. He owed them the truth, and maybe they could help him get out.

"I know where Kira is." The words tumbled from his mouth, and he was close to breaking down as he said them. He must have looked wobbly because Matt stepped closer, ready to catch Torin as if he was going to fall over, which he was close to doing.

"Tell me," Conner said through gritted teeth.

"I did something terrible," he whispered, looking straight at the cracks in the floor, cracks he and Kira used to jump over as kids.

Conner stepped closer and grabbed Torin's shirt. "Spit it out."

"It's okay, Torin. You can tell us," Matt said.

Torin reached for his elemer on his belt for support. "I used the hand of death on her. It was an accident," Torin said.

Conner's hand gripped his shirt tighter, shaking with white-knuckled rage.

"You did what?" Conner jolted him hard, but before anything happened, Matt and Dev pulled them apart and whisked them out the side door into the quiet hallway.

Torin slouched against the wall as Matt and Dev held onto Conner, but he slipped out of their grip. He pulled Torin up by his shirt, forcing him to stand up, and slammed him into the rough stone.

"Tell me it isn't real. Tell me she isn't dead," Conner spat in his face.

"It was an accident. I stopped her heart, but they started it again—Mrs. Young and Mr. Sampson. She was alive but hadn't woken up when I saw her last." The words came out jumbled like it couldn't be real that he was saying them.

Conner dropped his hand and smashed his fist into the wall by Torin's head.

Torin didn't flinch. He didn't even care if Conner hit him. He deserved it.

"I'm going to see her now. To apologize and say goodbye," Torin said.

"You bloody well aren't. Stay the hell away from her. You're the last person she'll want to see when she wakes up." Conner pushed Torin hard in the chest with one hand, then backed away, as if fighting not to punch Torin in the face.

That was probably true. She would never want to see Torin again, and he couldn't blame her.

"Wait. What do you mean say goodbye?" Matt asked.

"I'm leaving. What I did was wrong. What my father is doing is wrong, so I'm going to turn myself in and hope that I can find a way to make things right one day."

"You're serious?" Conner asked. The anger in his eyes dulled as he cradled his bleeding knuckles.

Torin nodded. He brushed off his suit, his arms feeling as weak and about as useful as noodles.

"Help me get out of here, and you won't have to put up with me anymore. Just promise you'll look after Kira. Make sure she doesn't piss off my father too much, yeah?" he said to Conner.

"Course we will," Dev cut in. "We can tell your dad you went to sleep. It's normal after taking the elixir, anyway. People will expect it. Right, Conner?"

Conner took a second to mull it over. He would be next to earn apprentice with Torin gone; he would benefit if he went along with this.

"I'm in," Matt said "If you can get out of here, maybe things can be different in the future. I'm not saying anything bad about your dad, but I'm sick of being in the dark, and I'm not so keen on being in a war if there is one."

Dev nodded, but glanced around. He was right to be paranoid.

"My life *would* be easier if you were gone," Conner said, running a hand through his hair.

"I just need to say goodbye to Kira. Let me do that," Torin said.

"Fine. We'll help you. But if Kira isn't okay, I'm coming after you. You know that, right?" Conner said.

"I'm sure you will," Torin said with a weak smile.

"This is nuts," Matt said. "You're a bloody lunatic, Tor, but we've always got your back. Remember that." He leaned in and hugged Torin.

"Go get on with it then," Conner said.

Torin said goodbye to his squad mates and didn't look back as he forced his legs into a run toward his room.

He unlocked his bedroom door and stumbled in, unable to get his sweat-soaked clothes off fast enough.

In the weak lamplight, he glimpsed himself in the mirror and did a double take. Unseen bruises had tenderized his skin, and he was sandblasted all over, but none of that showed. Instead, weaving around his right buttock and down his leg was a new tattoo, and the sight of it made him want to vomit.

It was the skeleton of a snake.

Its head rested on his butt cheek, and its skeletal body wound the full way around his leg, its tail stopping behind his knee. White lilies wove into its stark white skeleton, glowing faintly, so it almost looked 3D against his dark skin.

Why a snake? Were the gods taking the piss? Having a good old laugh at his expense?

He pulled on some black briefs and dark jeans to cover it up as quickly as he could. He never wanted to look at that again. Just what he needed, a constant reminder of this nightmare of a night burned into his skin.

He threw on his favorite *Star Wars* T-shirt and a black hoodie. At least he could turn himself over in comfort. Now the hardest part. Saying goodbye to Kira.

He slung his bag over his shoulder and didn't look back as he closed the door.

Chapter 14

T orin left the quiet hallway of bedrooms and skulked toward the service area. It was on the same floor but a long way when one didn't want to be seen. Clinking dishes and yelling gave away the busyness of the kitchen before he was even close. It was already into the small hours of the morning, but the feasting hadn't stopped. Checking his watch, he saw it was already 4 a.m., only a few hours from sunrise.

Pulling up his hood, he kept his head down as he entered the busy service hall. Trays of glasses and empty plates passed in one direction while platters of cheese, fruit, and finger foods passed in the other. Torin's stomach rumbled at him; he still hadn't eaten.

Passing the busiest point of the kitchen threshold, Torin let out a breath as he eyed the bedroom doors further down and made for the one next to Mrs. Young's quarters.

His chest constricted as he drew near. *Please be alive.*

"Skulking at this hour, Master Dumont?" Mr. Sampson said in the same way he did when Torin was a kid, then smiled when Torin turned around, probably looking like a deer caught in the headlights.

"I hear congratulations are in order," Mr. Sampson said.

Torin noticed how the older man's hair was all white now. When had that happened?

"I'm not sure about that," Torin said, knowing there was no point in lying. "I need to see Kira."

Mr. Sampson nodded in understanding. "I'm not sure that's wise. She isn't doing too well. She needs rest."

"She's alive, then?"

"She's alive," Mr. Sampson said, offering a small smile.

For the first time since this nightmare started, Torin found himself close to tears. The back of his throat tightened, and he bit the inside of his cheek to stop his lips from quivering. He let out a sharp breath and rubbed his face to snap out of it.

"I need to see her. I need to say goodbye."

"She isn't going anywhere. Come back tomorrow."

"Please." Torin was ready to beg or even cry if that helped.

Mr. Sampson spent an agonizing few seconds studying Torin and nodded to his bag before a smile crept to the corners of his thin lips. "I see. You've finally worked it out."

"What?"

"Seen your father for what he is, haven't you? You're leaving."

Was this guy a bloody seer or something? "I don't know what you mean." This could be another trick of his father's. Or a test. He was sure Sampson wouldn't tell his boss, but Torin wasn't willing to bet his future on it.

"Be quick about it then." Mr. Sampson gave a nod and opened the door, gesturing for Torin to enter.

"Thank you," he whispered. He blinked and ran a hand through his hair. *This is it.*

He nodded to Sampson and stepped into the room.

The small room was lit by a single lamp. Dull, yellow light spilled across the old-fashioned desk and dresser and crept onto the patchwork quilt covering Kira's too-still frame.

He wanted to believe it was the light that made Kira's skin so sallow and washed out, but he knew that wasn't true. He had done this.

Her hand rested on the side of the bed, her fingers so delicate and still, but he didn't dare touch her. He should probably never touch anyone ever again, knowing what he could do. An involuntary twitch in his hand made him jerk his own arm into his chest. Something dark inside pulled at him, almost willing him to pull the life from her once more.

He glanced behind him to see Mr. Sampson had shut the door. He was alone.

"I'm sorry, Kira," Torin whispered. "I know you'll never forgive me, but please keep living."

He couldn't keep it together anymore. He crumbled. Deep, uncontrollable sobs wracked his body as he collapsed onto the edge of the bed at her side. Burying his face in the quilt, he tried to block out the cruel ache that burned like wildfire in his chest. *How did everything go so wrong?*

He didn't know how long he stayed like that, but at some point, he became still. It felt like he'd been wrung out, like every ounce of energy had been sapped from him, and there was nothing left.

He sat up and rubbed his face. She lay there exactly the same as before, like Snow White lying in her coffin. But Torin wouldn't be the prince to wake her.

Spotting the water jug on the bedside table, Torin poured himself a glass. The cool liquid brought a little life back into him. He checked his watch; forty-five minutes had already passed. Too long. He needed to get out of here, before someone decided to check on him, and get as far away as possible by daybreak.

"I fucked up, Kira. I don't even know who to trust anymore."

His hands fell limp in his lap. It felt ridiculous talking to someone who was asleep, but this was the only chance he'd get to explain things to her.

"I won't be here when you wake up, but you should know I never meant to hurt you. I don't want to leave you behind, but I have to go, even if you don't understand why."

Next thing he knew, he was telling her everything. He told her about studying necromancy, about trying to bring Licorice back, his doubts about his father, and how he had concluded that he was a monster beyond help. He told her about everything that had happened that night.

"I'm going to make things right."

An alarm blared outside the room, and he sprung to his feet. This wasn't a fire alarm; it was the blasting sounds of air horns that indicated an attack. Torin glanced at Kira, but she didn't move.

Mr. Sampson rushed into the room. "Better get moving now before they block the gate to the garden."

"You're not going to stop me?"

"I overheard some of what you said in there. I know what happened to Kira."

Torin took a step back. "It was an accident." His hand slid to his belt; his fingers wrapped around the handle of his elemer.

Mr. Sampson raised his hands calmly. "I'm not accusing you, Torin; I'm saying that I understand."

Torin didn't let go of his elemer. Even if he left now, there wasn't much chance he would make it out via the Hollow. Guards would be stationed at all exits.

"You're a good lad, Torin, and the world needs to change. Becoming another version of your father won't help any of us, but if you find your own path, another way, things might be different in the future."

Yeah, different, like the world will probably end because of me. He realized how much he needed to hear something supportive.

"I'm going to turn myself in."

"Good luck. I have a feeling the world has a bigger purpose for you. But I'm sure your father won't see it that way."

"I'm sure he won't. How can you work for that arsehole?" Torin asked.

"He's not exactly someone you can walk away from."

Torin nodded. He understood that all too well.

"I'm going to try," he said with confidence that surprised himself.

"Better get going then. If you need help in the future, there are those of us who will remain loyal to you and to the House of Ravens. Things could be very different if you let them."

This wasn't something Torin wanted to think about. His immediate future looked too short to be planning anything else.

"Please look after Kira. Tell her how sorry I am, won't you?"

"Of course I will. Don't you worry about her. Go on now."

The sirens were doing Torin's head in; he couldn't think straight. Crouching down at Kira's side, he pulled his bag around and took one of Licorice's feathers from the front pocket, carefully tucking it beneath Kira's palm without touching her.

He hated saying goodbye and didn't understand why people were so inclined to say it all the time. Sometimes it was better to slip out unnoticed and without a fuss. But not this time.

"Goodbye, Kira. I promise I'll find you again. Stay strong." He kissed her forehead and stood up.

"I'm ready," he said to Mr. Sampson.

Chapter 15

Torin stepped out of Kira's room, and Mr. Sampson handed him the paper bag he'd been holding.

"Best of luck, young Torin," He patted him on the back and tottered off to join the stream of people leaving the kitchen.

There was a note on the bag. *You will always have friends here. -Mr. S.*

Torin opened the bag to find a water bottle, an apple, and a sandwich. He tucked it into his bag, already feeling a little less alone.

Torin didn't have time to waste getting emotional over a sandwich. He got moving and joined the stream of people heading out the back door of the kitchen. The alarms were even louder outside.

Perhaps he could still make it to the garden to get out via the Hollow. He sprinted across the driveway and darted toward the gates. Anders was standing there. Was he the only guard in this whole bloody place?

"Everyone is to assemble at the main gate," Anders said.

"Can you look the other way this time? I need to get through the Hollow now," Torin said.

"Boss's orders. No one in or out."

"Come on, Anders. Let me through." If he had to go join the others, they would see him with his backpack and non-formal wear. They would all know something was up.

"No offense, Torin. I like you, but it's your dad that'll have my head, so I'll be doing what he asks."

Course he would. No one would stand up to his father. That's what was wrong with this place, everyone living in constant fear. The other guard stepped in front of the gate next to Anders.

"I guess I'll be going to the front gate then," Torin said, pissed off, but he wasn't about to fight the two of them to try to get through.

Shit. Now what? The only reason they would gather like this at the gates was if someone was on the other side, waiting for them. It was either the House of Snakes or the Paranormal Justice Unit.

If it was the Snakes, it would be his blood they were after, and he would have to join the fight. If it was the PJU, he might have a chance to turn himself in. *If* he could just get outside without his father getting to him first.

Either way, he had no choice but to face the music and find out.

With shoulders back and a mask of confidence, Torin marched up to the crowded gates as if he had been planning on going there the whole time.

His father was already there, standing at the head of his small army, dressed head to toe in a black suit with that ridiculous cane at his side. Torin was the odd one out. At least he was also wearing black, but his jeans and a hoodie stood out, while most of the crowd were still in their formal wear, though some had changed into combat gear. He did his best to remain inconspicuous on the side of the pack.

"Take down these wards and come out and face me like a man, Korbyn!" a man bellowed from the other side. It was pitch black, but the lamps at the gate were just enough to make out the crowd. He guessed there were around sixty people on the other side.

Torin's father stepped closer to the gate, tapping his cane slowly as he went. His bandaged hand indicated he had already strengthened the blood wards.

"You are the one they call the Cobra, the Viper's brother, yes?" Korbyn said mockingly. "A hard one to track down, you are."

"You murdered my brother." The man's voice was barely controlled but sounded familiar.

"Your brother murdered my wife," Korbyn said bluntly. "But I'm afraid you've got the wrong man. I share my sympathies." He put his hand on his heart.

Torin stood with trained stillness as if that would help him go unnoticed. His brain stumbled, trying to come up with a logical escape plan.

Should I come forward now? Own up to this and get it over with? Or wait for the gates to open and risk a battle? He didn't want anyone else getting injured, but there was no clear path forward where people wouldn't get hurt.

The Cobra took out his elemer and blasted the gate with shadows. Probably to get some of his frustration out. As the man stepped closer to the streetlamp and the shadows cleared, Torin got a closer look at him. He knew the man. He was Mage Fletcher's partner. *Shit.* Mage Fletcher's partner was the Cobra? The Viper's brother? This wouldn't help him when he turned himself in. Which was looking like it would be very soon. He needed to figure out a way to get through the gate . . .

"Where is my son?" Mage Dumont called back.

Torin had nowhere to hide.

"He's over here," the man next to Torin yelled. *Turncoat.* To be fair, any of the others would have done the same. They had no idea how much of a traitor Torin was about to be.

Torin marched right up to his father and stood at his side, not looking at him but holding his back straight and his hands loosely behind him, all appearances of the confident soldier and apprentice. Beneath his façade, his throat was dry and his heart was racing like it wanted to escape his chest.

He trained his gaze on the man outside the gate who would probably kill him the instant he stepped outside. But if he gave himself up from in here, his father would punish him, probably disown him for the betrayal of his House. His options were not looking so good.

Finding a way out of the gates without bloodshed was his priority. The Hollow wasn't an option because of the wards within the grounds.

One thing he had up his sleeve was blood magic; he was one of the few people that could control the wards on the gates that were enhanced with good old Dumont family blood. Though he preferred to keep all his blood inside his body if he could. To do this, he would have to get closer.

Torin took a step forward.

"Back in line. Don't you dare think of talking to them, boy," his father barked.

Calling him *son* must have been a one-time offer only.

"Don't you want us to take credit for our work, Father?" Torin baited him.

Korbyn looked him up and down. "Not like this, you bloody fool. And why are you dressed like that?" He yanked Torin back by his bag into line beside him, frowning at the backpack.

But Torin knew what he had to do; he had a plan. A weak plan. But still a plan.

"It was me that killed him," Torin announced loudly, putting his hand up. He wasn't boasting; rather, he said it as a fact.

He looked the Viper's brother right in the eye, regretting doing so. The pain was unmistakable, but his gaze narrowed and quickly changed to fiery rage.

"Come out here and say that to me again," the Cobra yelled. He was right up against the gate now. Gone were the ball gowns and tuxedos from the party. Most were dressed for combat, all with elemers in their hands.

"What the hell are you doing?" His father gripped his arm tightly. "They've got nothing on you, no proof. Do not fuck this up." Then, in a louder voice, "Sorry Mr. Cobra, please disregard my son's comment. He thinks he's being funny. Still pissed from his birthday party you see." He gave a half-cocked smile as the men behind him all chuckled with practiced ease. *Suck ups.*

He would not engage his father; he had no chance of winning a fight against him, not when his father had far stronger magic and an army behind him. No, the only way Torin was getting through that gate was with diplomacy or trickery.

A head of red hair bobbed through the crowd and pushed through to the front on the other side of the gate. Torin let out a deliberately silent exhale. *Thank the gods.* It was Mage Fletcher.

At least she might control her partner if Torin made it out there. She reached the Cobra's side and said something to him that made him lower his elemer, but he didn't look happy about it. Now might be his only chance. He had to take it.

"Get behind me, you fuck-up," his father hissed at him.

Torin didn't move. Instead, he silently drew his elemer from his belt and bit into his cheek to stop himself from making a noise as he sliced across his left palm with the blade. Warm blood pooled in his palm as he made a fist.

This was it.

He darted out in front of his father and summoned a shield of shadows to protect his back. It wouldn't last long, just long enough to get through the gate. But he had to be fast.

His feet were in motion before his brain could react, and he headed straight for the gate, not daring to look around to see the reaction.

Blood pounded in his ears, and he blocked out everything. He didn't want to see what awaited him on the other side or what was happening behind him in case he failed. The cut on his hand throbbed as his pulse sped up.

The gate was only twenty yards away at the most, but it might as well be a marathon. Shouting and footsteps followed him, but his shadow shield held. He sprinted and didn't bother to slow down as he slammed into the solid metal. His bloody hand wrapped around the bars, and there was a burn of magic as the wards recognized him. He concentrated everything on his intention and told it to let him out. The gate clicked open.

But the ground fell out from under him as someone wrenched him back. Shadow ropes circled the back of his shield, digging into his shins, and flipped him hard. The shadows seized his ankle and dragged him. His belly scraped across the gravel, the fresh slice in his palm filling with all sorts of painful things.

So close.

Gripping his elemer, Torin flipped himself onto his back. He cut into the Shadow Dimension and summoned magic faster than he ever had before and sent a ball of shadows to his ankles to push and squeeze out the attacking shadow ropes. The attacker's magic was weak and easily broken. Not his father's.

He looked up and found himself at his father's feet. His stomach dropped, and he was a little boy again, terrified of a beating, but this had much higher stakes.

"You've lost your mind, boy," he barked and pointed his elemer at Torin's chest. This was his father showing his true colors. Torin knew he was doing the right thing. *Time to turn the tables.*

"My mind is perfectly clear, Father," he said, loud enough for everyone to hear. "You set me up. You tricked me, and you lied about the mission. I never wanted those people to die," Torin said. He stood up and brushed off his jeans, only pushing more grit into his bleeding palm.

"You did what you are trained to do. No more of this," he said, looking like he might strike out at any moment.

"Let me leave," Torin said. He had to give him a chance to do the right thing.

"No one leaves me. Not your mother, not you." His words were venom. Torin clenched his jaw and fought the terror that was building within him.

"She didn't leave you. She died, and you don't even care that her murderer is dead. I did that for you, and you didn't even blink an eye," Torin said, trying to keep the shake out of his voice.

In this moment, it was just him and his father.

The gate was too far to make a quick dash, and his father blocked his path out. New plan: get closer to his father. But not to use the hand of death; he'd never use it again, not even on this evil man who deserved it more than anyone. He had a new plan.

Flipping his bag around, he opened the front pocket and wrapped his fingers around the cool glass of the starbell toxin. He tucked it into his sleeve and grabbed a book.

"You can't beat me, boy. Don't even think about it."

"I don't plan to. I have something you might want." Torin kept his eyes trained on his father as he put his bag down and clutched the necromancy book to his chest.

"I doubt that very much." He smirked, but Torin could tell he was intrigued. If he wasn't, he would have attacked by now.

"I have *The Shadow Atlas*. If you let me go, I'll give it to you."

"You do not."

"I have it, Father. Do you want it or not?" He held up the back of the small black book. It was actually *Necromancy Through the Ages,* but he was betting on the fact that it was similar enough to his father's descriptions of *The Shadow Atlas* to pass for it.

"I could take you out now and make you look like the fool that you are."

"You wouldn't do that to your own son," Torin said, not believing a word of it but wanting everyone else to hear. If he was leaving, he wanted his memory to be one that opened a few people's eyes to the truth.

His father pursed his lips into a thin line. Torin pulled out the water bottle Sampson had given him and opened it and held it over the book.

"I hear magical books don't like water."

His father tensed. His eyes locked on the book with genuine fear. There was something to this; he almost wished he had the real book if it was worth all this trouble.

Tension hung in the air. The men were waiting for the command to attack, and so was he. People at the gates were shouting, but he blocked it all out.

"Give me the book and you can go."

Torin almost laughed. *He wasn't that stupid.* He knew this man too well, and he had no intention of letting Torin go.

"Deal. I will now hand you the book and then walk back toward the gate."

His father nodded, hands resting graciously on his cane.

Torin stepped forward. He dropped the water bottle and held the book with white-knuckled force at the same time he maneuvered the tiny bottle in his sleeve and popped off the cork, careful to keep it upright.

Moving closer to his father, he reached out his hand to shake on it. His father was a man of traditions. No matter what he thought of Torin, a deal couldn't be done without a handshake. Torin was counting on it.

The gap closed between their palms, but at the last second, he tilted the bottle, pouring the contents onto his father's bandage-covered palm and careful not to get any on himself.

His father realized too late. He flinched and flicked his hand away, shaking it.

The men stood still, waiting for instructions and looking confused. They hadn't seen the vial.

"Somebody get a healer!" Torin said as his father fell to the ground, and he dropped the vial, crunching it into the gravel with his boot. Torin leaned over him and let his father see his smile of triumph. "Stay back. I don't know what happened," Torin called back to the men, and surprisingly, they believed the concern in his voice and obeyed.

Torin put his departure off a few extra seconds. He couldn't help but relish the look in his father's eyes, knowing he had bested him.

Leaning in close so it looked like he was helping his father up, he watched as his limbs froze into temporary paralysis and his magic ebbed away, leaving him defenseless.

"Goodbye, Father."

Korbyn's face twitched with the strain of trying to speak. "I offered you everything. You're a coward, just like your mother," he rasped, trying to catch his breath.

Torin froze. Another one of his tricks, knowing it would hit him where it hurt. Somehow, he continued to fight the toxin.

"Want to know a secret, boy?"

"I'm sure I don't," Torin said, ready to back away.

He grabbed Torin's shirt and pulled him in close. "I killed your mother," he whispered. "She made me weak. She was going to betray me." A gurgle sounded in his throat. He was laughing.

Torin's breath froze in his chest. *It couldn't be true.* Torin's hand naturally moved to his father's chest, and it took every inch of Torin's strength not to use the hand of death on him now. It would have been so easy, too easy. His hand shook with the force of holding back.

"You're a monster," Torin hissed.

His father's grip tightened on his shirt. His fingers were freezing up, and Torin wrenched them off him and stumbled back. He glanced around. Everyone was too far back to have heard anything and too afraid to come closer. Torin didn't blame them; it was safer to wait for the healer.

"That's what happens to people who get in my way, and you'll pay for this, boy," Korbyn whispered as his lips froze up, so quietly that no one else could hear.

"No. I'll make sure you pay for this," Torin leaned in and whispered in his ear.

Torin stood up as Mrs. Young rushed over, puffing and panting.

"What's happened?"

Torin did his best to keep it together. He'd just found out he'd murdered an innocent man for nothing, and his father must have been the devil himself to have treated his son this way. There was no hope for redemption.

"It was starbell toxin," Torin whispered to Mrs. Young as he tucked the book into his jacket pocket and walked straight toward the gate. Nobody stopped him.

Chapter 16

Torin's blood hissed against the iron as he creaked open the gate and stepped through.

Despite walking toward a potential attack and certain detainment, he had never felt freer. With slow steps, he moved through the crowd of his father's enemies. It was like a dream, but unlike a dream, he couldn't change the outcome; there was no dream weaving in the real world. No escape from what he had done.

Mage Fletcher let out a heavy sigh with a slight shake of her head as if she didn't want to believe it was true. She was the only person who had tried to help him, to offer him a way out. He felt like he'd let her down, despite not even knowing her.

She stood in a defensive stance with her elemer in one hand and nursed the embers of a glowing fireball in the other.

Torin stepped up to her. No one else moved, their eyes crawling over him like cockroaches.

She paused, carefully weighing her words before speaking. "Torin Dumont, do you confess to committing premeditated murder at the House of Snakes Manor?"

Torin nodded. "Yes. I did it."

Murmurs erupted around him, loud and angry. He focused on her but gripped his elemer, watching out of the corner of his eye in case anyone jumped him.

"And do you confess to setting explosive devices in ten locations within the house?"

Torin nodded. "Yes," he said calmly. As he caught the Cobra's eye by accident, Torin's heart squeezed in his chest. The man didn't look mad anymore. His eyes were red, his body slumped with grief.

How did everything change so fast? Yesterday, Torin had wanted nothing more than to destroy this man's family; he had wanted them to feel the pain he had felt, for them to lose someone they loved like he had. But seeing it in real life brought him no satisfaction. He wished he could take it all back.

"Torin Dumont, you are under arrest and under the protection of the Paranormal Justice Unit to determine justice as we see fit."

Mage Fletcher grabbed him at lightning speed. He didn't speak as they ripped his elemer from his hand and his backpack from his shoulders. Her hands were hot with lingering fire, and she wasn't gentle as she cuffed his hands behind his back. It was clear she wanted to do this quickly.

In a second, he saw why as she shoved him through the crowd.

"You can't just take him," a man shouted.

"We have a right to our own justice!" said another.

"They can't keep getting away with this!"

"They're monsters!"

The rumble of protests grew louder, and Torin felt the loss of his elemer as if he'd lost a limb. Mage Fletcher looked around, presumably for her partner. He appeared at her side, eyes still wild and hands balled into fists at his sides. It was clear he was fighting his own instincts not to kill Torin. Torin remained calm and quiet, not wanting to do anything to antagonize this man or the others. That's what they were waiting for.

"Back off!" the Cobra yelled at the crowd. "I will make sure we get justice."

"You're one of them now! How can we trust you?" a woman shouted.

"Because I'm the head of this House now, so you'll bloody well listen to me." He turned his back on them. "Let's get out of here," he said to Mage Fletcher, who was already following as he stormed off.

Morning light filtered through the gaps in the curated trees that lined the road. The sky turned a muted gray as a raven squawked in the distance, and Torin glanced back at the Rook. It stood the same as ever, solid and unmovable against the changing sky. He didn't know if he'd ever be back.

They threw a bag over his head, and everything went dark.

They traveled through the Hollow. He could taste the familiar biting cold on his tongue and inhaled the welcoming chill of the still air, even through the bag.

They dragged him out of his sanctuary to have the familiarity replaced with the stink of coffee and old carpet. The sound of keyboards clattering away, printers whirling, and the low drawl of chatter told him he was in some sort of office. He imagined some dingy police precinct like the ones on TV.

The noise dulled as they pulled him along in the darkness, his breath growing hot and moist against the bag as he did his best to stay calm, but slow panic was creeping over him with every step. *If I confess to everything, they have no need to torture me, right?*

His father had told him horror stories, and he had witnessed enough torture at the Rook to know how to avoid it. With that in mind, he still had every intention to cooperate.

He had turned himself in so he could make a difference.

Someone ripped the bag off, and bright fluorescent light seared into his retinas. He blinked and tried to get his bearings as someone shoved him into a hard plastic chair.

His eyes watered, struggling to focus. Through the blur, he made out a metal desk, two chairs, one exit, and no accessible weapons. Two figures came into focus—Mage Fletcher and the Cobra.

"Archmage Norwich is on her way," Mage Fletcher said and left the room without making eye contact with Torin.

This can't be good. Norwich? He scoured his memory. She was from the House of Owls—their specialty was mind magic.

Why was the Archmage from the House of Owls coming? Surely, he wasn't important enough to bother the higher-ups.

The Cobra sat opposite him, and Torin tensed up, ready to take a blow as the man leaned in. But the hit never came. The Cobra leaned back in his chair and crossed his arms, unmoving and glaring at Torin.

It was clear he didn't want to sit still. The next minute, his white-knuckled fists pressed into the table.

Torin took a slow, calming breath.

"You're a real piece of work, you know that? By the time the Justice Unit is done with you, you'll be wishing you were dead."

Torin didn't reply. He didn't want to make this worse.

"That's when I'll be waiting," the Cobra said in a low, calm voice.

A shiver ran down Torin's back. He didn't want to show how highly unsettling that statement was. "I'm sorry. I know that can't mean much to you, but I am."

Torin didn't try to explain why he did it; that wouldn't help bring the man's brother back, and by the looks of him, he was so on edge anything might set him off. But it was the opposite. The man crumbled before his eyes. His staunch demeanor and hatred evaporated in a split second as his façade broke down.

Torin sat there in stunned silence at the sudden change. He wasn't trained in emotions. He was trained in actions and reactions. Reflexes and fighting. He twisted around, wanting to get away and wringing his hands still in the handcuffs. Glancing to the side, he stared at the flaking white paint on the door, hoping that someone, anyone, would come back into the room. Even the Archmage. Anything was better than this.

"He had a little girl. You took him away from her, you monster."

The Cobra rubbed his forehead hard with both hands. It was obvious he was fighting to get his emotions under control. Torin didn't breathe as the man regained his composure. When he looked up, he stared past Torin with blank eyes.

Torin's heart threatened to smash into a thousand pieces. He thought this was what he wanted. How could he have been so blind as to sentence a girl he didn't even know to a life without a father? What sort of revenge was that? He hadn't even deserved it.

"I'm sorry," he whispered, and he meant it. But he knew it meant nothing to the man.

Without warning, a switch flipped in the Cobra's eyes, and he exploded. Torin ducked his head as the table flew past him and smashed against the wall.

"He didn't deserve this!" Shadows streamed from his elemer and circled Torin's neck, throwing him hard into the wall, twisting and crushing his windpipe. Time stood still, and he saw this could be the moment it was all over. He deserved it.

A rush of air blasted across his face.

Torin gasped for a breath, his lungs screaming and his throat burning. He crashed down from his suspension on the wall.

He was up in a flash, arms still behind his back, ready for another attack. But none came. His rescuer waltzed across the room. It was the old man from the House of Snakes party, the one who had tornadoed up the broken glass. He must have blasted away the shadow, and if he was here, that was good news; obviously, he hadn't died, so maybe others had gotten away too.

Mage Fletcher ran in and shoved her partner hard in the chest. "You're a fucking idiot. How was that supposed to help?"

"It made me feel better," the Cobra growled as she pushed him out the door.

He didn't blame the bloke at all. He would have done the same if it were Kira.

The weather mage gave Torin a serious nod, then left. Mage Fletcher set the table upright and helped Torin back into his chair.

"You're in deep shit. You know that, right?" she said as she set the other chair back on the other side.

"I know, but I plan to cooperate fully."

"Good. But why? Why did you turn yourself in?"

She had the right to be skeptical. Torin sat up straight and looked her in the eyes, wanting her to know he was serious. "I'm here with an offer. I want to stop my father, but I need help."

"You turned yourself in, admitting you murdered someone, and now you're asking for our help?"

"We want the same thing. You offered me help before; admittedly I was stubborn and needed to learn the hard way. But I know the truth now. I've seen my father for what he truly is. There is no saving him."

"The hard way? People are dead because of you. You know that, right?" Mage Fletcher said.

"Yes. I know, and I feel horrible. I want to make it right." He kept his face blank, pushing his emotions down so he wouldn't break down and become a useless mess.

Mage Fletcher's nostrils flared. "You can't make it right! You think you can waltz in here, give some crackpot apology and ask for a deal to get you off by ratting out your dad? It doesn't work like that, Torin."

He could see how this looked bad. "I'm not asking to get off anything, you can lock me up forever for all I care. I just want to stop my father from hurting anyone else."

"Oh." She shuffled in her seat, then wrote something in her notebook. "Let's start with why you did it."

"I thought the Viper killed my mum. My father told me it was him; he set it as my test to become an apprentice. I never thought for a moment he didn't kill her. I'm a fucking idiot for never seeing it. I never worked it out." He shook his head, wanting to bash it against a wall. There was no excuse. He had followed instructions blindly instead of using his brain—this is what he got.

"And the explosives?"

"I didn't have a clue about that. Honestly. He set me up. I thought I was planting bugs."

"I see." She wrote in her notebook again, giving nothing away. "You feel guilty?"

"Yes." *Of course I do. Why the hell would I be here otherwise?*

"And you want revenge? You want to take him down? What is it?"

"I don't want revenge. I want to stop my father because he's dangerous." He looked up, trying not to get frustrated, and was met with a warm smile.

"We agree on something there. You can call me Danni."

"Why are you being so nice to me?" he asked.

"Because I believe everyone deserves a second chance, and I had a good feeling about you the first time I saw you. I knew you weren't like your father."

There was a hidden sadness behind her eyes, but she seemed genuine.

Someone knocked on the door. He sat up straight as a slight woman with a bob of pure white hair marched in. She glared at him through pale blue eyes and stood by Danni's chair, causing Danni to jump up as if she'd been electrocuted.

So, this was the Archmage. She sat, and Danni drifted behind her to lean on the back wall, looking like she wanted to melt into it.

The woman's cane had a carved owl's head, and she reminded Torin a little too much of his father for his liking. If she used her mind magic on him, he would be no match. He was too weak to conjure even a basic shadow shield, and she was probably one of the most powerful mages in the country.

"I hear you are a competent shadow mage," she stated in a posh accent. "Is it true you can perform the hand of death?"

"Yes, it's true." He wouldn't lie. She would know.

But it didn't matter because, the next moment, a searing light beamed into his eyes, as white-hot as the sun, but worse was the mind-crushing pressure he couldn't escape. She yanked his memories from him, flashing them across his vision like a terrible movie he could do nothing to stop.

Time stood still and appeared endless as days, weeks, years of memories were heaved up and thrown back at him. Everything was forced to the forefront of his thoughts for this vile woman to see, and she saw everything: Kira, Licorice, his training, his childhood, his mother, his life, and everything from the last twenty-four hours. He was too weak and too low on energy and sleep to even try to fight it.

Suddenly, it was over. The blinding light blinked away, and for a moment, the world was a comforting pitch black as he crumpled to the concrete floor.

His head pounded like it might explode, and he had no strength to get up. One thing in his future was sure: he was going to learn how to block mind magic so this never happened again.

"I have everything I need. Let us discuss." She nodded to Danni, and they both left the room.

Torin dragged himself up and rested his head on the cool stainless steel table, letting the chill of the metal take the burning out of his forehead. He wasn't sure how long he lay there; he might have fallen asleep, because dreams of the horrible events of the night were stamped onto the forefront of his mind. Either that, or he was delirious from the mind scramble.

"I shall offer you a deal, Mr. Dumont." A voice and a blur hovered over him like a hazy angel of death.

He groaned and forced himself up.

"I relayed the events from your mind to Mage Fletcher, and she will offer you a reduced sentence of between five and ten years if you promise to aid the Paranormal Justice Unit with information about your father and the inner workings of the House of Ravens. You will also agree to serve me during your incarceration, as well as after you are released. I have need of your skills for a particular job."

"What skills?" he asked. He sounded drunk; he was so messed up from her magic that he couldn't even think enough to string more words together.

"Your shadow magic, specifically the ability to travel by the Hollow."

"Not the hand of death?"

"No. That would be illegal," she stated. Though he had a feeling legality was something that wouldn't stop her from doing anything.

"Good." His eyes closed against his will. *So sleepy* . . .

"Or think about it this way. You'll be locked up for fifty years if you don't agree to my deal. Take the offer, and you can have everything you want."

His eyes wouldn't open again, and his forehead fell to the table. Everything went black.

He didn't know how long he slept. But he must have needed it. He awoke in a cell on a wooden bench with a scratchy gray blanket on top of him. There were no windows, the walls were white brick, and there was a steel toilet-sink combo in the corner of the room.

Danni was already at the door as if she'd known he would awaken.

"I left your lunch next to the bed. Don't tell the Archmage," she said.

Torin groaned and sat up. The scrunched-up paper bag Sampson had given him sat on the floor by his feet. When he spotted the sandwich, he realized how hungry he was. It had been so long since he'd last eaten. He scoffed down the sandwich and the apple, then had enough energy to focus again. Maybe Sampson was a seer after all, because that was the hungriest Torin had ever been in his life.

Danni was still at the door.

"Take the deal," she said, almost panicked. "If you don't, you'll never get out."

"But won't there be a trial?"

"No. She wants you, and she always gets what she wants. So just do it. She's not lying. It's a real second chance."

"Why do you even care?"

"I've seen what she can do, and we need more shadow mages who aren't on your father's side. You can help us."

At least she was honest. He was useful, and that was what it came down to. The problem was, he didn't deserve a second chance. This offer seemed too good, and he couldn't use a get-out-of-jail-free card. He needed to be punished.

"What would I have to do?"

"Sign a contract saying you will train in whatever she deems fit, and you are to work for her when you get out. You will also tell us everything you can about your father and the House of Ravens. That's all you have to do. Here, read it."

Danni shoved a wad of paper through the bars, and he sat there for a good ten minutes and scanned over it twice.

"She wants me to train in archeology and do research? It seems too easy. What's the catch?" She must have seen his interest in history in his mind—creepy.

Danni shrugged. "Hey, I just work here, but from what I understand, she wants you to use the Hollow to collect relics around the world for her."

"Like steal them?"

"I'm sure she prefers to use the terms liberate and reunite."

"So, I'll be in prison training to be a criminal?"

"Or you could choose to look it at as becoming re-educated, getting a degree in archeology, and having training privileges most other inmates do not have."

"Oh." That sounded good. Too good. He was still going to prison, but he was sure Danni's partner wouldn't be happy about it. He would probably kill Torin when he got out anyway, the whole "that's when I'll be waiting" thing.

How could he trust any of these people? He supposed he had little choice at this point, and this was why he had come here. At least this way, he could take down his father.

"Can you tell me what happened to my mother? Do you know?" He would see if she lied to him now.

"This isn't going to make you feel any better, Torin."

"Just tell me. Please,"

She took in a deep breath that wasn't very reassuring. "There is no evidence that the Viper killed your mother. We believe he was trying to protect her."

Torin's chest squeezed tight. So, it was true. Despite all the signs staring him right in the face, he just hadn't wanted to believe it. But he had to accept the truth. She continued.

"There was a fight. The Viper, as you call him, had a very different account of events. He said your mother was running away. That she wanted to start a new life away from your father's oppression. The House of Snakes had been helping her leave—she had friends there. She left that morning, and your father found out where she was. She thought she could reason with him, so she went out and met him at the gate. But when Korbyn saw she couldn't be talked back to his side, he grabbed her and took her into the Hollow. The Viper went in after her."

Danni avoided looking Torin in the eye. He sat there with a sickening feeling in his gut, knowing where this was going.

Danni swallowed. "The Viper came out, and your mother was dead in his arms. Apparently, there was a fight in the Hollow; she got stabbed with her own elemer. He said your father did it, but there was no proof, and they ruled it as suicide."

"Before the Viper died, he said my mother wouldn't have wanted this. I thought he was trying to trick me. But he was helping her." Hot tears stung at the corners of his eyes but didn't fall. This made things so much worse. He had been a good guy, his mother's friend, even. But another darker thought crept in. When his mother left, had she planned on coming back for him? Or did she abandon him with his father, knowing what he truly was? He wasn't sure he wanted to know.

"I'm sorry, Torin. It didn't make sense for him to kill her if he had been protecting her. She left your father and wanted help to disappear, to start a new life. A lot of people can vouch for that. I'm sorry to be the one to tell you this, Torin. But we believe the person that murdered your mother was your father."

"Don't be sorry. He told me himself right before I left; he said he killed her because she made him weak, because she was going to betray him. Can you believe that? I thought all this time he loved her, that he was so sick with grief he turned into this other person. But it was all a fucking lie. Why is he like that?" Torin spat, suddenly wishing he had used the hand of death on his father.

"He's insane. Just take the deal, Torin. It's your chance to do something about it. You'd be stupid not to."

She was right. The problem was he was going from being under his father's thumb to slipping right under the Archmage's.

He nodded. He couldn't think about this anymore. His brain was so hot and overloaded to the point where he was ready to shut down. "Yes, I'll do it," he said.

"Good. Just so you know, there will be a 'public trial,'" she said with air quotes. "And you'll get a minimum five-year sentence for show, but you'll be studying and training under the Archmage's regime during that time. She saw something in you she needs; that's all it is. Don't mistake it for generosity or kindness. She can just as easily leave you to rot if she changes her mind," Danni warned.

"I deserve much worse than this. I should be locked up forever for what I did." It was so much worse now knowing he had killed the man who had helped his mother. His father was even worse for tricking him into doing it.

"You're probably right. But you are *so* young, Torin. You can still learn and undo whatever rubbish they taught you."

He took the pen Danni was holding out.

At least five years in a "reform camp." That was all it was. Of course, there was the downside: the public trial, the negative press, and pretty much everyone from every single magic House hating him forever. A lifetime of rejection and punishment—that would be his real sentence.

They would limit his magic and watch his every move. But if it led to taking his father down, so be it. It gave him a reason to want to live.

"If I sign this, can you find out what happened to my friend Kira? She's still at the Rook, but I want to make sure she's okay."

He might never see Kira again, but he hoped he could make her life a little better in the future if he could change things.

Danni gave him a pitying look. "I'll do my best."

He put the pen to paper and let the black ink sink into his rolling signature.

"Why do I feel like I've just sold my soul to the devil?" he said without looking up.

"Because you have," Danni said, her voice laced with sadness. "But I've got your back."

Epilogue

Seven years, eight months later

The interrogation room, like all the others, was floor-to-ceiling white tiles, no windows and nowhere to hide anything. Torin was well aware of the drill, and clasped his hands in front. The cold handcuffs pinched his wrists as the guard jammed them on and latched them to a ring on the table. He had no choice but to sit on the plastic chair.

The guards were dicks. They thought themselves tough because of their elemers and magic. If Torin wanted to, he could take down any of them without his elemer.

But he'd never tried and had no intention of doing so.

Most of the people in the prison . . . sorry, *reform camp*, didn't believe Torin could use the hand of death or that he'd even murdered anyone. They mostly left him alone because they knew who his father was. No one would risk messing with him. Plus, he had grown in the last seven years and eight months.

Torin felt both the same and different from when he went in. His hair was the same as before, shaved close to his scalp, but he was much bigger than when he'd first arrived, big enough to take care of himself in any fight. But he only continued his combat training out of routine and for fitness.

He still had the same goal he'd never lost sight of—taking down his father. He had given the Paranormal Justice Unit every detail he knew about the House of Ravens and his father.

But they had yet to get anything to bring him in on; the devious bastard was too careful and used others to do his dirty work. Everyone knew the House of Ravens was growing stronger, but no one seemed to be able to do anything about it. Torin didn't have much faith in the PJU anymore.

Once he was out, he would be the one to do something, but when that day finally came, he would try diplomacy first. He would find a way that didn't involve killing. He had been patient so far; what was a little more waiting?

He had trained hard and kept to himself as much as possible. Focusing on his studies and research for the Archmage kept him busy most of the time, and training in the same cold and miserable patch of mud every day kept him strong. Secretly, he had also taken the time to study mind magic—specifically how to block it.

So, he sat there in that room perfectly still, waiting for the door to open and for someone to give him another bullshit excuse about how long he would be in here. It had been years since he had seen the Archmage. She was leaving him here to rot.

If he was lucky, it would be Danni who came to see him. As the least annoying of his handlers, she actually treated him like a person. She'd been the one to keep him focused on his studies when he couldn't see the point. She'd been the one who convinced the Archmage he could have one day out to attend his graduation, and she'd been the one who forced him to take his mage's tests early, both tests. He owed her everything, and because of her, he was one of the youngest azurite-level mages in the country.

Tapping his fingers on the cold table, he fought the urge to seek ambient magic and draw it in. It would only make it worse. He hadn't used magic in a week, and his fingers buzzed, craving it. It was torture not having his elemer. Even so, he had it better than most.

As one of the few who had the privilege of regularly practicing magic in a secure room, Torin was one of the lucky ones. It was a secret, of course, but the type of secret everyone knew, and it was the one thing that had kept him sane all this time.

Most of the inmates hated him for it. But without it, he would be just like the rest of them, tortured by building up magic, slowly driving them crazy.

The door swung open, but Torin didn't look up.

"Not even a greeting, Mr. Dumont? Have they broken you at last?"

Torin swiveled around at the sound of the Archmage Norwich's voice.

"Not likely," he said, and sat up a little straighter.

"Good. I have need of you."

The back of his neck prickled. *Was this it?* He didn't want to get his hopes up. The way she said it certainly didn't sound good. But she was here; that had to be a good sign.

"I am pleased with your time in here. You have not demonstrated the psychopathic tendencies we expected to see in you. Instead, you remained focused and levelheaded while excelling in your studies. I am impressed with the research you have completed so far."

High compliments from the dragon woman herself. Though she still sounded displeased about it.

"Thank you, Archmage." Personally, he didn't think it was that impressive. He literally had nothing better to do than focus on studying and building up his magic every chance he got. What else was he going to do while he was locked up?

"I am both concerned and impressed by your advances in Shadow Magic. It's clear your father's monstrous training methods have some merit. Azurite mage at twenty-three; impressive."

Impressive, yes, but for what? He might have outstanding qualifications, but he had lost seven years of his life. Seven years of growing up and being a normal young adult. He didn't know how to talk to people anymore. He'd never had a girlfriend. He was twenty-three and afraid of going out there again, afraid they would be afraid of him.

The Archmage continued, "But as you can see, I am here now, which means we are at a point where we must proceed with the mission. I should like the relics all together in the next year."

"The next year?" he said, overly politely. *She must be joking.* Seven years of research and he had barely scratched the surface of thousands of years of records with only hints and clues. Plus, he needed to do field research before he could pinpoint where the hidden relics were in the world.

"Yes. It seems we have run out of time. We are no longer the only ones tracking them."

He refused to react; just clenched his fist and chose not to smash it into the table. Why hadn't she gotten him out sooner?

"I see," was all he could think to say. He was going to have to do some serious bullshitting to make it look like he could find them if this was his way out of here. He might track down one or two, at the most, but there were twelve relics, and several had been missing for thousands of years. The Archmage already had a few, which was a good head start, but not nearly enough.

"I trust you understand the importance of this. We cannot let them fall into the wrong hands."

"Yes, they could destroy the world," he said. *Obviously.* She was well aware of this, and hopefully, her reason for collecting them was to prevent this very outcome.

Knowing his luck, it would be his father after the relics, thought he also didn't trust the Archmage as far as he could throw her. She might be a bitch, but he judged her at least sensible enough not to want to destroy the world.

Either way, he would have the time to work it out before the collection was all together.

"Mr. Dumont! Are you even listening? I have filed the paperwork to let you out today," the Archmage snapped.

He sat there blinking, staring at his hands. Was she being serious?

"Out?" He hadn't even had time to mentally prepare.

"Don't make me regret it." She clearly wasn't impressed with his level of gratitude.

"Thank you, Archmage. I won't let you down."

She let out an unimpressed huff. "When you are settled, we shall meet to discuss your plan. I must be going now."

She left, and Torin sat there trying to comprehend what had just happened. He was going to be free . . .

Torin looked back at the white electric gates as a bracing wind swished through the yellow grass in undulating waves. He was out. He was on the other side of the fence, standing next to Danni at the top of the cliff with the churning blue and white sea below them. It was the fourth time he had left the compound in nearly eight years. Danni grinned at him like a proud mother duck, linked her arm with his, and gave his wrist a squeeze. He did his best not to flinch. He wasn't used to people touching him. But she had been as good as her word; she'd always had his back.

Danni placed his elemer in his hand.

"Would you like to do the honors of taking us home?"

Home. A foreign term.

"You're not worried I'll get us lost in the Hollow?" he joked.

"Nah, you'll be right as rain. Plus, the mage who dropped me off left, so you have no choice."

"Where is home, anyway?" He expected he'd be going to some halfway house, or a dingy basement, to work for the Archmage for the next year as some sort of archeology/shadow mage slave. Though the contract said he would get paid; he had no idea if that was true.

"To the Tower of London. I expect you know where that is?"

He bit back a groan. The Tower of London; headquarters for the House of Owls, the biggest community of mages in London—small, crowded with tourists, and full of people who hated Shadow Magic.

"Is staying in prison an option?" He looked at her with a twitch of a smile at the corner of his mouth.

"Oh, come on, it's not that bad. It'll be nice for you to be around people again. Maybe find a girl . . . catch up on lost time." She winked, and Torin raised his eyebrows.

"I'd prefer to be alone, thank you. And I know where the Tower is." Knowing Danni, she'd already have blind dates set

up for him, and he didn't need to be a seer to know how that
would go.

"Well, what are we waiting for? Slice away," she said, grinning.

He shouldn't complain. But if this was where he was heading,
he was in for a stressful reintroduction to society. He took in a
deep breath and ordered his hand to stop shaking.

"Don't worry, love, it won't be that bad, and the Archmage
allocated you a secure tower so you can work in peace. Plus,
you'll be living near me and my family! We won't let you starve."

Starving was the least of his worries. Getting stoned to death
at the Tower now seemed like a legitimate concern. But he trusted Danni. She had become closer than his own family. He owed
her everything and would do anything the woman wanted to try
to make it up to her—though he suspected he never could.

"Right, let's get a move on."

"Wait. Have you found anything out about Kira? Do you
know where she is?" Torin asked.

Danni's shoulders slumped. "Sorry, love. Same as before.
We've followed up on all the leads we can on her. Still no records
of her death, so there is a good chance she's alive, possibly working as an operative for your father."

Torin nodded. Danni had done everything she could to find
Kira. The truth was, dead or alive, if his father wanted to hide
someone, no one was ever going to find them. He had to let her
go. He liked to think she was a powerful shadow mage out on
undercover adventures around the world. His delusions made
him sleep a little better at night.

"Tower of London, here we come," he said with a forced
smile as he cut into the Hollow, and Danni followed behind
him. The sharp smell of ice and winter that haunted the Hollow
washed over him as he stepped through. Cool blue light filtered

over Danni's pale skin, making her look rather corpse-like. He wished he could stay in this bubble.

He cut another slit into the darkness, dreading what would be on the other side. But it was time to move on. Time to make things right.

Stepping out from behind a hidden wall, they appeared near a side entrance of the large fortress wall near the River Thames. The blare of a truck horn and the chatter of enthusiastic tourists was deafening. He inhaled a lungful of car fumes, coffee, and muddy river smells. Danni smiled and sidled up next to him.

"Welcome to the Tower of London." She linked arms with him, and they stepped into the crowd.

Also By Jenny Sandiford

The Shadow Atlas Series

  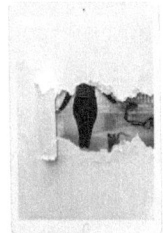

Acknowledgments

I had a lot of fun writing this book, which was originally going to be a short story, but somehow turned into a novel. I enjoyed discovering Torin's backstory, and I hope you did too! This is just the beginning of Torin's journey, and you can see plenty more of him in the rest of *The Shadow Atlas* series.

Thank you, wonderful reader! I hope you enjoyed this taste of *The Shadow Atlas* world and come back for more. If you would do me the favor of leaving a review on Amazon and/or Goodreads, I would be so grateful.

I would like to thank my husband, Michael, for his love and unending support, as well as his ability to listen to me ramble about scenes and characters. He is the best help in fixing scenes and plot holes, even when he had no idea what I'm talking about.

A massive thanks to my two critique partners Bethany Arliss and Liz Highland, both are wonderful fantasy authors who read the early versions of this book and made it so much better!

Especially big thanks to Bethany, who keeps me sane in this strange author world. Her support in all things publishing is a lifesaver and sometimes it's just nice to have someone in the same boat there alongside you. Thanks Bethany!

Thank you to Liz for making my writing so much better, and for continuing to teach me about grammar (I suspect this will be a lifelong journey lol).

Thank you to my mum, Maggie, for her love and support with writing and all things creative, and thanks to my sister, Lucy, for being my biggest encouragement to write books.

A massive thanks to everyone who helped make this book happen: my wonderful editors Mandi Oyster and Lori Diederich, proofreader Amy McKenna, and cover designers Miblart.

For all those ARC readers, bookstagrammers, and anyone who helps share my books on social media or by word of mouth, you guys are awesome! You have no idea how much it means to me, and how much it helps. Thank you.

Thanks again for reading! See you in the next *Shadow Atlas* installment.

About The Author

Jenny Sandiford

Jenny grew up in small town New Zealand on a steady diet of fairytales and fantasy books. She lived in Mongolia for nine years with her husband where they spent the unfrozen months of the year living on the edge of the Gobi Desert mining gold. When she isn't writing, Jenny enjoys hiking, meeting new animals, and loves to curl up in a sunny corner with a cup of tea, a cat, and a book. She lives in Darwin, Australia, with her husband and their two street cats from Mongolia.

CONNECT WITH JENNY ON:

Website: jennysandiford.com
Instagram: instagram.com/JennySandifordAuthor
Facebook: facebook.com/JennySandifordAuthor
Goodreads: Jenny Sandiford

WANT THE LATEST BOOK RELEASE NEWS?
Sign up for monthly updates!

jennysandiford.com/subscribe